MILE-HIGH DEATH

A Tess Winnett
Novella

LESLIE WOLFE

PRAISE FOR *MILE HIGH DEAD*

"Intense and worth the read Tess is a great character and can pull you into the storyline the entire series is great"

"Leslie Wolfe has written another great Tess Winnett novel. The plot and the characters were extremely well developed and kept the story going at a fast pace."

"Have enjoyed every one of Ms Wolfe Tess Winnett series. Looking forward to the next novel in this remarkable series. Thanks!"

"FBI Agent, Tess Winnett amazes again. It was hard to put the book down for fear I would miss something. Then I realized I was reading instead of watching. Can't wait for Ms Wolfe's next book."

"Awesome. Love this series. So good. Love how this character doesn't take any crap and gets the job done. Great read."

PRAISE FOR LESLIE WOLFE

"Leslie Wolfe never fails to amaze me with her stories!! Fast paced, her WOW factor of her characters and the crimes they investigate never disappoint!!"

"I follow Leslie Wolfe's books and enjoy them immensely. This was no exception."

"I love anything by Leslie Wolfe. Her books start with a bang and they end with a bang with no cliffhangers. Her books flow seamlessly from one book to the next"

"Leslie Wolfe always turns out a good read! Just enough twists and turns to keep you guessing and then then gob-smacked by the ending! Loved it."

"Leslie Wolfe always provides the reader with a suspenseful, page turning thriller! I continue to look forward to all of her new releases!"

BOOKS BY LESLIE WOLFE

STANDALONE TITLES

A Beautiful Couple
The Surgeon
The Girl You Killed
The Hospital
If I Go Missing
Stories Untold
Love, Lies and Murder

TESS WINNETT SERIES

Dawn Girl
The Watson Girl
Glimpse of Death
Taker of Lives
Not Really Dead
Girl With A Rose
Mile High Death
The Girl They Took
The Girl Hunter

DETECTIVE KAY SHARP SERIES

The Girl From Silent Lake
Beneath Blackwater River
The Angel Creek Girls
The Girl on Wildfire Ridge
Missing Girl at Frozen Falls

BAXTER & HOLT SERIES

Las Vegas Girl
Casino Girl
Las Vegas Crime

ALEX HOFFMANN SERIES

Executive
Devil's Move
The Backup Asset
The Ghost Pattern
Operation Sunset

For the complete list of books in all available formats, visit:
Amazon.com/LeslieWolfe

MILE-HIGH DEATH

A Tess Winnett
Novella

LESLIE WOLFE

$\varprod$ **ITALICS**

Italics Publishing Inc.

Edited by Joni Wilson.
Cover and interior design by Sam Roman.

ACKNOWLEDGMENT

A special thank you to Mark Freyberg, my New York City authority for all matters legal. Mark's command of the law and passion for deciphering its intricacies translates into zero unanswered questions for this author. He's a true legal oracle and a wonderful friend.

1

FLIGHT

Her heart swelled as she stepped on the heated tarmac. She almost didn't look at the cabbie, while the old and disapproving crab handed her the wheelie with the laptop bag affixed on top. His watery eyes shifted from her beaming smile to her slim figure and then to the slick Gulfstream G650ER waiting with the cabin door open. The sight of the business jet brought out a scoff, followed shortly by a clucking of his tongue, none of which he made the tiniest effort to disguise.

Her smile withered just a tiny bit. She hated being judged by anyone, more so by this cog in the transportation machine, someone who, if he didn't watch it, risked forfeiting his tip.

"Anything wrong?" she asked, ready to give him a piece of her mind in a tone he'd remember for a while, even if it seemed he'd already started grappling with senility.

He just scoffed again and extended his hand, anticipating payment for his service. She obliged, shaking her head slowly, and deciding she wasn't going to let him ruin her mood. Who did he think he was, judging her like that? How did he know that jet wasn't hers to begin with?

She breathed with ease the moment he drove off, leaving her alone on the tarmac, wheelie handle in hand, only some forty yards from the idling plane.

Her beaming smile returned in full force.

She couldn't believe what was happening to her. Experiences like these never happened to girls from Rapid City, Iowa. Only yesterday, after yet another endless sales presentation conducted under the fierce eyes of her boss and the initially indifferent looks of the client, she'd thought she'd have to return to Miami crammed in an economy seat by her boss's side, enduring crappy conversation, spiced with occasional lewdness and permanent halitosis.

But no . . . a late-night delivery of flowers and champagne, delivered in white gloves straight to her hotel room, had accompanied a handwritten note on luscious white cardstock.

"*Experience life my way,*" the note read, and she mused over each letter, breathing in the words that brought butterflies to her stomach.

The white-gloved man waited respectfully by the door, and when she looked up from the note, he delivered his instructions.

She was invited to fly home to Miami in Richard's personal jet, departing from the Houston Executive Airport at noon, or whenever she'd like. Due to concerns for his privacy and to keep the media vampires at bay, she was kindly asked to wear a hat and sunglasses on her way to the airport and refrain from speaking to anyone about the invitation. Mr. Sanford would be delighted to share Miss Lambert's company. He was also regretful he could not join her for dinner that night. Nevertheless, he had made arrangements for her and would be thrilled if she would say yes.

She couldn't find words; her throat, constricted by emotion, barely allowed her to nod and utter her approval. Then she quickly grabbed her purse and checked her looks in the mirror.

Enchanted, she followed the young man downstairs to the restaurant, stepping quickly and quietly on her stilettos, the sound of her heels smothered by the plush carpeting of the luxury hotel. She was surprised that Brad, her boss, had sprung for such a nice stay; probably he'd matched their travel budget with the size of the prospect he was trying to impress.

The man held the door for her as she entered Mastro's Steakhouse, an exquisite culinary landmark she didn't have a travel budget for. It didn't seem to matter, when she was led directly by a smiling hostess to an entire area that had been cordoned off, keeping curious guests at bay.

A single table was set on an impeccable, white damask cloth, a white rose in a tall, crystal vase marking its center. Another card leaned against the thin, tall cylinder.

"*Myra, have dinner with me,*" the card read, "*at least in spirit if not in person. Until tomorrow, we can only dream.*"

Her moist eyes lingered on the letters spelling her name. He had a way with words, she had to admit. He was unparalleled at making a girl feel special, and she'd almost forgotten she'd overheard Richard order three dozen roses for his wife as a wedding anniversary gift. Okay, so he wasn't going to be hers forever; he was married. Bummer . . . but still.

She stopped reminiscing and filled her lungs with the hot and humid air, loaded with hints of jet fuel and exhaust, and the scent of sweltering asphalt under the summer sun. She approached the jet, wondering what the trip would be like. How Richard would be.

She was ten yards from the plane's door when he appeared at the top of the steps, as breathtaking as she remembered him from yesterday's excruciating overview of Southeast Chemical and Paper product offering and special terms for high-volume contracts.

There was a ruggedness to his handsome features, an intensity in his eyes that brought butterflies to her stomach, anticipating the moment he'd touch her skin, leaving searing traces where his fingers would wander. When their eyes met, a spark traveled through her entire body and stretched her lips in an excited smile. She playfully tilted her head to the side and stopped, waiting for him to close the distance.

As he did, his eyes tensed, while traveling her body from head to toe and back. He lingered a little where the hem of her tight skirt touched her thighs, then found the curves of her full breasts, where the silk of her white blouse exposed her tan skin.

Without a word, he grabbed the handle of her wheelie, his eyes locked with hers, intense, a sense of dire urgency conveyed in the directness of the gaze, so dire it prickled her skin with goosebumps and brought a flicker of a frown to her forehead.

She followed him, nevertheless, her hand melting in his firm grip, letting him lead her aboard the idling aircraft.

"Where would you like me to sit?" she asked, finding herself flustered and hesitant all of a sudden, an unfamiliar feeling for her. She'd always been brave, unyielding, determined. That's how she made it out of Iowa and had built a life for herself in Miami, as an account executive for a Fortune 500 company. But this man had a perplexing effect on her. She seemed to be subdued entirely to his will, as if she'd lost the ability to think for herself somewhere between the flower and champagne delivery last night and the solo dinner that had followed.

He closed the aircraft door and locked it, then laughed, turning to face her. He grabbed her hand with a playful smile that didn't reach his tense, dark eyes.

"It's just the two of us, so, wherever you like."

She swallowed, feeling wary, as a chill traveled down her spine.

"How about the pilot?" she asked.

"You're looking at him," he replied, his low voice eager, the same urgency coming across in the way the words were spoken. "Why don't you join me in the cockpit?"

Her full-bloom smile returned, while her uneasiness dissipated. She'd never seen the inside of a jet's cockpit before.

She followed his lead and took a seat by his side. He fastened her seatbelt, his hands brushing against her body and sending waves of excitement through her heated skin. He helped her put on her headset, his fingers getting caught in her long, wavy hair. Not by accident, she was sure, and the thought of that brought another round of butterflies, just as he was getting cleared for takeoff by the Houston Executive Airport tower.

"You've completely ruined commercial flying for me," she said playfully. "How will I ever be able to do my job, flying economy at least two times a week?"

He just grinned, looking at her for a long, loaded moment. Then he refocused on his controls, flying the plane without a word. Tension had tightly clenched his jaws, muscles knotting under his skin. She wondered why. There was something off about him, his reactions to seeing her, to her being there with him, in that tight space, all alone with him in the sky.

He touched a few controls, and then released the buckle of his seatbelt.

"Autopilot's on, and we're free to move around the cabin," he said, his voice a bit colder than she'd heard him speak to her in her dreams.

She followed him toward the back of the plane and managed to smile when he offered her a glass of champagne.

She dipped her lips in the chilled liquid. "How long is the flight?"

He abandoned his glass on the small table and touched her

hair. "Long enough," he replied with a waning smile. He took the glass from her hand and led her to the back of the plane, her hand numb in his tight grip. When he stopped and looked at her, his gaze chilled the blood in her veins. His eyes were cold, dark, and lusting with an intensity she hadn't seen before. For a brief and illogical moment, she thought of screaming and running away, but who would hear her, and where would she go?

Somehow, between yesterday's magic and today's reality, her dream had turned into a nightmare.

She forced her lungs to draw air and her hands to stop shaking.

He opened the door to a rear compartment that had been lushly decorated as an inflight bedroom and led her inside, his grip on her hand just as merciless, his gaze intensifying with unspoken menace.

She tried to pull back, but he easily held her in place, not releasing her wrist. The corners of his mouth flickered with a smirk as his left hand gently caressed her long, dark hair, softly playing with the curls, while his eyes drilled into hers.

"Please," she whimpered, too scared to think straight. "I—"

He grabbed a fistful of her hair and pulled down forcefully, forcing her head back. Then he ripped her blouse off with a quick gesture, leaning over her with a grin of lustful and merciless anticipation.

She screamed until her lungs were empty of air, then drew breath and let out another shriek, her wails covered by the jet engines and his laughter.

"You and I are going to have so much fun, my darling Gen," he said, undoing his zipper. "You'll finally get what you really want."

Stunned, she stared into his deathly eyes. "My name's not—"

He slapped her hard across the face. He licked his lips as he watched her eyes tear up and the blood stain her swollen mouth. He tasted that bit of redness while his hands traveled lower on her body, unyielding.

"Oh, my darling, *darling* Gen," he whispered in her ear, his voice menacing, an evil foreboding that chilled her to the bone. "I've been dreaming of this moment since the day I met you."

Against all reason, she screamed.

2

BODY

Tess approached the cordoned-off area with a raised eyebrow and muttered oaths, quickly making her way past the emergency vehicles with the flashers on, through dozens of onlookers and media people frantic to get a quote or a shot of the victim, anything to fuel the masses' lust for blood and sensation. A couple of news helicopters were circling the area, always hungry buzzards eager for some fodder.

"Agent Winnett," a familiar voice called from the crowd. "Tess!"

She stopped and turned, searching the crowd for the face that went with that voice.

"Mr. Rusch," she acknowledged the man holding a microphone with a local TV station's logo. "You've moved up in the world, I see. You switched from investigative journalism to the world of fake and scandalous drama," she added, unable to refrain from smiling.

"A man's gotta eat," he replied unfazed. "But my heart is and always will be in investigative journalism," he added, lowering the foam-padded microphone. "Which is why I have to ask, what's going on here?"

She touched his shoulder briefly in a gesture of camaraderie. They went back years, and on occasions, he'd proven helpful and a good resource to have by her side. "I'll tell you everything I know so far." She paused, giving him time to start his camera, while a glint of amusement lit her eyes. "I woke up, had my coffee, and got called to assist with a new investigation."

"Wait . . . What? That's it?"

"I just got here, Mr. Rusch. And I'm not psychic."

Deflated, the man lowered his camera and ran a weary hand against his receding hairline. "I thought you were down with calling me Brandt."

"Okay, Brandt, but I still don't have anything else to share. Now, will you please excuse me?" She walked away quickly, waving off the approaching horde of frustrated journalists.

Tess flashed her FBI badge, and the Collier County deputy posted by the perimeter lifted the yellow tape with a quick head nod. She slowed her pace, allowing herself time to take in the details.

A wide section of the Naples beach had been cordoned off, keeping all tourists at bay. A few yards from the shore, a Coast Guard vessel had dropped anchor, and several Coasties were getting ready to bring a body to shore. Waist deep in clear, turquoise waters, Doc Rizza instructed them in a loud, slightly raspy voice.

Tess put her hand up to shield her eyes from the piercing sun. In the distance, bright red Coast Guard helicopters were flying in a search pattern. If she squinted hard, to the point of tearing up, she could make out several WaveRunners searching the waters, also in a search pattern.

There was another vessel at anchor, as close to shore as it could possibly reach, a fifty-foot yacht with two people onboard and an incessantly barking retriever pacing the deck. The woman had wrapped herself in a blanket, despite the afternoon heat, and the man stood by her side in a protective stance, as if the Coast Guard and all the law enforcement swarming on the beach were a dire and immediate threat to their lives.

"Hey," she heard a man say, "thanks for coming."

She shook the hand extended and then hugged the Palm Beach County detective. "Boy, did you wake up on the wrong side of the peninsula today or what?" she asked, stepping back and looking at him with scrutinizing eyes. He'd aged a little more since she'd last seen him, maybe added a couple more pounds around his waistline, but he was the same old Gary Michowsky she knew well. Driven, cunning, and overall, one hell of a cop. But stubborn as a mule.

"Nah," he replied. "We were all called in to lend a hand with the search. But the moment I heard what they found, I knew I had to bring you in."

"And the local sheriff is okay with that?"

"More than okay. Elections are up in less than a month. The last thing he wants is an unsolved murder case to bring his numbers down. He's only got a few years left until retirement, you know. He'd gladly fork this over to Palm Beach if he could."

She chuckled. "Yeah, like that's going to happen."

"Right," Michowsky replied.

"So, talk to me. Why am I here?"

"Remember a few years ago, when you told me you only needed one victim to see that it was the work of a serial killer?"

She nodded. "Sometimes you can see the signs of that psychopathology from the first victim who is found. It's apparent in the manner of death, in the killer's ritual. But usually, there are more than one. We rarely have the luck to catch serial killers before they kill for the second time. If we only have one, it means we haven't found the others yet."

Michowsky scratched his buzz-cut hair. "Well, I believe this vic fits the bill."

"Have you seen the body?" Tess asked, seeing how the

stretcher was being unloaded from the Coast Guard vessel, a forty-five-foot lifeboat. "When?"

"They heloed us over to the site, a hundred and fifty miles out," he replied.

"And CGIS didn't claim jurisdiction either?" she asked, furrowing her brow. Last thing she needed was a territorial fight with the Coast Guard Investigative Service or another agency. That would go extremely well with her boss, Special Agent in Charge Pearson.

"No," Michowsky replied calmly. "I made a strong argument, and they agreed to hand it over to you. And me, by association," he added, with a trace of excitement in his voice.

She laughed quietly, her eyes still riveted to the stretcher that was being slowly carried to shore on the shoulders of several Coasties. "What was that argument, if I may ask?"

"That they're not equipped to handle this case. I presumed they've never seen a case like this, and they had to agree."

Doc Rizza had reached dry land and directed the men to set the stretcher on the sand, a few feet from where the gentle waves washed ashore.

She started walking toward Doc Rizza, and Michowsky followed. "What are they still looking for?" Tess asked, pointing at the Coast Guard helicopters, barely visible in the distance.

"Any witness, anyone who could've seen or heard anything."

"And those two found the body, I'm assuming?" she asked, shifting her gaze toward the yacht. "Wait, don't tell me, their dog barked at something in the water?"

"Exactly," Michowsky replied. "The woman unloaded her lunch the moment she saw the floater."

"She contaminated whatever evidence was left?"

He nodded. "Yup. Barfed all over the vic."

"Great . . . just great. How far out there were they?"

"One hundred and fifty-two miles, due west."

"That far, huh?"

She kneeled next to the stretcher and greeted Doc Rizza with a quick smile. If time had been merciless with anyone in the past few months, that was the coroner. She knew he'd been struggling since his wife had passed, choosing to spend his nights at the morgue instead of his empty house, and opting for liquids instead of solids for dinner. She found herself staring at him for a good couple of seconds while making a mental note to visit him one day when they were not on a case.

"They called you, huh?" Rizza asked. "The moment I saw the body, I thought they should."

He slowly unzipped the black body bag, careful not to disturb whatever trace of evidence might still have lingered on the body. Water, especially salt water, is a great forensic countermeasure, washing most bodies clean of all trace evidence in only minutes.

Doc Rizza finished unzipping the bag and opened it. Tess approached the girl's body, focusing on her face. She hadn't been in the water too long; the bloating that irreversibly disfigures submerged bodies had not yet started to show.

Tess used a gloved finger to gently remove wet strands of hair clinging to the girl's face. Her beauty still showed, despite the bruising on her jaw and a swollen left eye. Her lips were slightly parted and pale, the lower lip a little swollen and showing some indentations and a deep split.

"What are these?" Tess asked. "Bite marks?"

"I'm going to say yes, although I will need to confirm it back at the lab." Doc Rizza sighed. "See this split, here? I'll go out on a limb and say she was hit across the face and that busted her lip, but then she was bitten hard, multiple times. Some of the bites broke her skin. See here?"

Tess didn't reply. She stared at the girl's arms, apparently tied behind her back. But something else had caught her attention.

Every bone in her naked body seemed to have been broken or crushed in multiple places. As Doc Rizza cut the cable tie that held her wrists together, her arms settled in unnatural positions. Her legs were the same, bones broken but no visible bruising. Where her wrists had been bound, deep lacerations stood in testimony of her struggle to escape, to survive.

"Any signs of sexual assault?" she asked, lowering her voice as if the media sharks could hear her from the edge of the perimeter.

He nodded. "It's a strong possibility, from what I can tell without having her on my table."

"How long has she been dead, Doc?"

"I'd say no more than three to five hours. The Gulf waters are warm and have delayed the onset of rigor, but I'm also not seeing major signs of wildlife activity on her body. Usually, fish and birds go to work after the skin has started to decay. But there are cutaneous changes of immersion present." He looked at her and added a clarification. "Her extremities are pruned."

"Can you give me a cause of death?"

"She shows signs of strangulation and the associated petechiae," he said, pointing at some bruises on her neck. "She didn't drown, I'm certain of it," he replied. "She was floating shortly after death, meaning that it wasn't the decomp gases that held her body to the surface; it's too early for those. It was the air in her lungs. We were lucky to find her. A few more hours and she would've dropped to the bottom."

"Why?"

"She was found face down, which trapped the air in her lungs and prevented it from being replaced with water. A stronger wave to flip her face up or just the passing of time would've allowed enough air to escape and her body to lose its buoyancy until decomp gases would've brought it back to the surface again."

"I see," Tess replied, "but I'll need more. What killed her, Doc?"

He sighed heavily, straightening his back with his left hand propped against his side.

"If I were to venture a guess, which I never like to do, is that she fell from high altitude. See all these broken bones? That happens when you hit the water at high velocity. It's like hitting concrete, only without the skin lacerations that come with the rough surface abrasions. I've seen this type of trauma in high-speed water-skiers."

"Yet, you're assuming she fell from up high?" Michowsky asked. He'd kept quiet for a while, a permanent frown digging ridges on his forehead.

"Yes, I'll venture a guess that she wasn't water-skiing naked with her hands tied behind her back," Doc Rizza replied.

"That's not what I meant," Michowsky said, sounding a little flustered. "I'm not an idiot. I was thinking she could've been thrown from a high-speed boat. Some of these multiengine types can easily go seventy knots."

"Got your point," Rizza replied. "I'll clarify that after I examine the fracture lines. Dropping from above doesn't have the same twisting effect that being thrown from a fast-moving vessel would have. Think of stone skipping. If thrown from a boat, her momentum versus the water surface would show in the manner her bones broke. I'll let you know."

"So, if you were to venture a time of death, Doc?" Tess asked, knowing how much the coroner hated making imprecise statements. He'd mentioned three to five hours earlier, but she wanted to confirm.

"I'd have to say it was sometime between eleven A.M. and two P.M. today. I'll know more after I finish the autopsy."

Tess peeled off her gloves and shoved her hands deep inside her pockets. She stared at the vastness of the Gulf of Mexico, wondering through what miracle the girl's body had been found.

The odds of that happening were nonexistent.

The killer had made sure of that.

3

MARRIED

At twenty-three, Richard thought the world was his. He was the single heir of a billion-dollar industrial conglomerate. He was tall and ruggedly handsome, and he was charismatic. The sports cars he loved to drive, in total disrespect for posted speed limits, were additional girl magnets, but he proved to be hard to get, although many coeds had tried and failed. For some obscure reason, it wasn't that easy to get into Richard Sanford's bed, not even in his silver Porsche.

Drawn to his good looks and his family fortune like moths to the flame, many girls attempted the impossible. Some even ignited a glint of interest in the young man's eyes, but he always chose to walk or drive away on his own. Few had noticed the clenched fists and tensed jaws when he did so. Yes, he could have them all if he wanted, but it wasn't smart to give in to his urges. And he had the willpower not to light the fire he knew he couldn't control once it was kindled.

Nonetheless, life was good for him.

He'd just graduated cum laude from Yale School of Engineering and Applied Science, and his hard-to-please father had thrown a relatively decent party for the occasion, complete with a couple of girls who didn't say no to anything he demanded, to compensate for the many times he'd refused the advances of his coeds. Come midnight on that day, his father had presented him with a formal job offer delivered pompously in a wax-sealed, gold-lettered envelope.

He was to join Sanford Industries as the vice president of

sales, on a direct path to someday taking over the reins of the company from his aging father.

Yeah, the bastard was aging all right, but not nearly fast enough. He had stamina and drive and was relentless about the business, about every minute of Richard's time. He expected Richard to give his everything to the family business, just as he had.

And so, one day, Richard came home to find his perfectly architected world was about to change.

The old man was seated in front of the study fireplace, sipping twenty-year-old scotch from a cut crystal glass and wearing cigar smoke like a halo around his balding head. On the opposite chair, a somewhat older, heavier, and more obnoxious version of his father sat with his legs crossed and a greedy grin on his face. The two men could've been brothers.

"Richard," his father had said, "have you met Mr. Wilkes?"

He promptly approached the guest and shook the hand that was offered, ignoring the cigar ash the bastard sprinkled on his shoes.

"Of Wilkes Consortium?" Richard replied with a wide smile that managed to look sincere. "No, I haven't had the pleasure yet."

That's how his slavery had started, with a stranger in his father's study, the stench of Cohibas, and a handshake he'd never forget because it had sealed his fate. He still remembered that night, the sense of uneasiness he had experienced seeing how his father fawned over Wilkes and knowing he wasn't privy to the whole story. What were the two tycoons up to?

That story started unfolding shortly thereafter. In a private conversation happening behind closed doors, his father, with an unyielding stance and a firm tone of voice, had announced

Richard's engagement to Wilkes's daughter at the same time he informed his son about his intention to merge the two companies into Sanford Wilkes Enterprises. "It makes sense," he said, blocking his son's objections with a hand gesture and a raised baritone. "We're the biggest heavy equipment manufacturer; Wilkes is number one in steel. Times have been hard while you've been partying at Yale. Not just for us, you know. All American manufacturers struggle."

"But, Dad—"

"There are no buts here. Your wedding date should be sometime before August. Now, go see your future bride. Her family is expecting us on Sunday for the official proposal of marriage. Just a small circle of friends, nothing big. About two hundred people or so."

"Dad—" he tried to plead, but he couldn't get a word in.

"Not another word, son," the old man said, letting himself fall heavy in his burgundy leather armchair. He looked older all of a sudden, tired, drawn.

Richard crouched in front of his chair to be on the same eye level. "What's going on, Dad?"

The old man sighed and lit another cigar. "We need this to happen. Our cash flow's been taking a beating for years now. We have become dependent on steel imports at high prices. If we want to survive, if you want your legacy to be worth more than a pile of junk, we need this alliance to take place and be sealed with more than signatures on a contract."

He found himself at a loss for words. He wanted to swear, scream, strangle the old man with his bare hands. After all, mergers could be signed without having to marry someone. That was so last century.

"She's not that bad, son," his father added, as if reading his mind. "You don't have to love her." He blew a cloud of bluish smoke in the air, sending it twirling above Richard's head. "She's totally fuckable, you know? I'd marry her myself if her old man would allow it," the old man added with a raspy, lewd laugh that morphed into a coughing spell.

Maybe Geneva Wilkes *looked* fuckable, but was she, really? Richard's needs were special, leaving him with little choice but to seek the company of women who were willing to satisfy his intense urges without objections.

The moment he'd seen Geneva, he knew those urges were to be denied, confined to the darkest recesses of his lusting body when he shared the bed of his wife, kept under the strictest control. The classy, snobby socialite, who hadn't even agreed to take his name, was an ice block in bed. She probably had the same enthusiasm for their union as he had. Noticing that, he was relieved to see he could visit with her less and less often, and she voiced no complaints, apparently, preferring to sleep with her Löwchen dog Althea than with him. Even the dog was a pretentious little snob; apparently only a few remained in the world and had been the dogs of choice for Chinese emperors, at some point or another in their spoiled history. The mutt looked like a regular, fluffy canine accessory to him anyway, and Geneva could've gotten a dog looking just like that from the local pound.

But that pretentious furball and his wife's low libido had brought him the freedom to spend his nights at will, as long as he was discreet about it. And that he was. He'd learned the need for discretion the hard way.

Their marriage evolved well in the first couple of years, if what they had could even be called a marriage. But one night, after an exquisite meal and a certain bottle of Pineau des

Charentes, a sweet French wine with unexpected consequences, he made a drunken pass at his wife, and she didn't send him away. Maybe she was just as horny as he was, after sipping two glasses of that intoxicating elixir. They held hands all the way back from the Palme d'Or restaurant in Coral Gables, and they almost tore each other's clothes before reaching the bedroom door.

Lust and wine swirled in his heated body, fueled by Geneva's eager moans and undulating body, and soon he forgot all about his need to control his urges. Overtaken by dark passion, he tied her hands and smothered her screams until he found his release. He hadn't noticed that halfway through his assault, she'd stopped fighting him, choosing to stare at him with cold eyes, waiting for it to be over, the determination in her gaze as steeled as her family's roots.

Lying spent and grateful by her side, Richard had removed her restraints and placed a kiss on her cold lips. "Baby, you were amazing," he'd whispered, still oblivious to her deathly stare.

She got up and wrapped a silk robe around her body, then rubbed her sore wrists for a long minute, staring at the naked man lying in her bed. Then she turned away and left without a word.

The following day, she was waiting for him in the living room when he came home. Seeing her icy glare, his smile died on his lips while worry unfurled in his gut, setting off alarm bells.

"I knew who you were before we were married," she said, going straight to the point without any introduction. "You don't think I was going to marry a total stranger without a full background check, did you?"

She waited for him to reply, but he stood frozen, slack-jawed.

"Baby, what are you talking about?" he managed to ask, but his voice was trembling pitifully.

"You gave me some nice souvenirs last night," she added, showing her bruised wrists. "But don't worry, my dear," she added, her voice dipped in poison. "These will heal. That's why I have taken photos of every bruise you left on my body and placed them in safekeeping with my lawyer, in case some unforeseen accident would happen, and I'd be hurt in any way."

He swallowed hard, as he started to comprehend where this was going.

"Now, let's discuss the new terms of our marriage, my dear husband."

She paused again, expecting him to agree. All he could do was nod, his teeth too clenched to allow any spoken words to come out.

"I'll keep it simple. You do what I say, when I say, how I say. That includes everything, even sex. You are not to lay a single finger on me without permission, ever again." She smiled, seemingly savoring his humiliation and prolonging it. "If you break this arrangement, the photos will come out, and with them, the entire dossier my investigator put together on your youthful indiscretions."

A jolt of fear traveled through his body. How much did she know?

"Yes, that dossier includes the girls you raped at Yale. Remember those poor creatures? Did you know one of them needed hospitalization? Did you even care? How much did your daddy fork out to make them go away?"

She stood and then picked up her fluffy mutt, quickly placing a smooch on the dog's nose with a smile and a happy flicker of love in her gaze. Then she faced him, her eyes turned steel-cold again.

"Welcome to your new life, hubby dear. May it be a long and painful one. If you had any self-esteem, you'd shoot yourself."

Minutes after she'd left and closed the door, his jaws were still clenched so badly he didn't feel the pain from the molar he'd cracked while grinding his teeth to keep himself from killing her right where she'd stood.

He was screwed for life. The damn bitch from hell would never let him go.

But one day he'd be free.

4

AUTOPSY

The coroner's office was a familiar place that came with the territory of being an FBI agent, the type most frequently assigned to investigate murders, especially those where Tess's profiling background was a valuable asset. Yet every time she set foot on Doc Rizza's domain, Tess shivered, the coldness of the room more imaginary than real, enhanced by the metallic furniture, the steel tables, and the body freezers aligned on the back wall.

He'd been up all night, working, she'd concluded upon receiving his text message at five-thirty that morning, inviting her to review preliminary findings. Michowsky had received the same message, but he'd managed to squeeze in a coffee stop on his way in and approached with a spring in his step while carrying a tray with three tall paper cups bearing their respective names scribbled in blue Sharpie.

The smell of the freshly brewed coffee collided with the strong chemical odors in the morgue. The strongest, formaldehyde, prevailed and made Tess crinkle her nose and decline the coffee offering.

"Maybe later," she said, then approached the lab table where the coroner worked. "Good morning," she greeted him with cheer in her voice, then added, catching a whiff of sweat mixed with traces of alcohol. "Or, should I say, good evening, in your case?"

"Clinically speaking, morning refers to the time of day, not to my chosen lifestyle," he replied, not taking his eyes off a screen, while he adjusted some samples under the digital microscope's lens. "So, it's good morning until noon," he added, looking at Tess with unapologetic, bloodshot eyes surrounded by dark circles.

"You could've slept last night," Tess admonished him gently.

"Do you know how lucky we were to find this girl so soon after she'd been killed, in the Gulf of Mexico? It's almost twice the size of Texas!"

Tess nodded. "Still, you could've—"

"Could've what?" he cut her off, rubbing his nape thoroughly. "Could've gone home to enjoy an evening with my family?" The bitterness in his voice was heartbreaking. "At least here I can do some good."

"I—I didn't mean it like that," Tess replied. "You still need rest."

"And I didn't mean to be a jerk," he said, avoiding her gaze. "I know your heart is in the right place." He walked toward the autopsy table with slow, heavy steps. "Let's just focus on her instead, shall we?"

"Do we have an ID yet?" Michowsky asked, seeing a driver's license pulled up on one of the monitors. "Was she reported missing?"

"Again, we were lucky. No missing persons report yet, but her fingerprints were in the system. She was a frequent traveler with TSA clearance." He bent over the keyboard with a quiet groan, and the driver's license filled the large screen. "Meet Myra Lambert, twenty-nine, from Palm Beach."

"Huh," Michowsky replied. "She's from my jurisdiction. I knew there had to be a reason why I got involved in this case."

Doc Rizza gazed at him with a mix of curiosity and amusement. "Since when did you become a predestinarian?"

"A what?" Michowsky asked.

"One who believes that events are predestined or fated to happen a certain way."

"How did she die, Doc?" Tess asked, unable to take her mind off the young woman's demise. Only yesterday, she'd been Myra Lambert, a young and beautiful woman, full of life, smiling, living, thriving. And now she was nothing but a lifeless body, covered with a white sheet, cold as death on the coroner's table.

Michowsky had set up his laptop on the lab table next to the digital microscope. He typed slowly, using only the index and middle fingers from both hands.

"She—" Doc Rizza started, but Michowsky cut him off.

"She was a project manager, working for Southeast Chemical and Paper. It's a big company, over five thousand employees," he said, after clicking through a series of screens. "Wow, I didn't expect that," he added.

"Didn't expect what?" Tess asked.

"Look at her," Michowsky said, his face flushed red. "I thought she was a high-end escort or something."

"Really?" Tess reacted, her voice a bit higher that she'd wanted. "Just because a woman is beautiful and sexy means she can't have a brain or use it to make an honest living?"

"No, that's not what I said," he rushed to explain. "Statistically, in South Florida, when you see girls like her, they're usually not project managers. I'd say more than ninety-nine percent of them aren't."

Tess let out a frustrated breath of air. She was still angry but had to admit Michowsky had the numbers by his side.

"Let's focus on the preliminary findings for now," she said, approaching Myra's body.

The coroner peeled back the white sheet that covered Myra's body and exposed her head, neck, and chest.

"As I had suspected, there was far more under the surface than meets the eye," he said, directing their attention to the screens mounted on the wall.

"Underwater?" Michowsky asked, visibly surprised.

"Under the skin surface." He displayed a series of photos in hues of blue. "Under certain wavelengths and using a special camera, we can visualize bruises that haven't had the time to form and discolor the skin. Sort of like seeing tomorrow's bruises today."

Tess squinted and approached the wall screen, trying to understand what she was looking at.

"All the dark spots and stains are bruising not yet visible to the naked eye. See here?" he added, pointing at a view of Myra's neck. "She was strangled repeatedly, with bare hands, like this," he added, demonstrating on Tess's neck but without actually touching her. "He was facing her, strangling her multiple times, his thumbs pressing hard on her windpipe."

"Are we talking sexual asphyxiation?" Michowsky asked.

"That term in my book implies consent, but yes."

"There's no way this was consensual," Tess replied.

"I agree," Doc Rizza said. "There's extensive bruising on her arms and legs, her inner thighs, and her buttocks. But that's not what killed her. My guess is he choked her on and off until she fainted, and he must've assumed she was dead. But the official cause of death on my report will be ruptured aorta due to a high-velocity fall."

"From where? A plane?" Michowsky asked.

"That's your job to find out, not mine," Doc Rizza replied with a tired smile. "Mine is to tell you her preliminary tox screen was clear, and that she was sexually assaulted, forcefully and repeatedly. No DNA, though, no trace evidence of any kind, but that's not uncommon for floaters."

Tess stared into emptiness. "My mind's still processing the high-velocity fall in the Gulf of Mexico. How on earth did that happen?"

"My first guess is with Michowsky. She must have fallen, or better said, been thrown from a plane," the coroner said, taking a seat on a four-legged stool and rolling it closer to the lab table.

"Despite what they show in movies, cabin pressure makes opening a cabin door mid-flight impossible," Tess replied. She spoke slowly and quietly, her mind still gnawing at the one detail that didn't let her think of much else. Had there been any other victims?

"Yeah, I believe that's true for a jet," Michowsky replied, "but what if it's a Cessna, or something small, flying low?"

Tess frowned, trying to visualize how the assault could've happened in a Cessna.

"Not unless he raped her someplace else and only flew to dispose of the body," she offered. "But how can you move a body in the middle of an airport, in broad daylight? In a suitcase, maybe?"

No one replied for a long moment.

"Maybe he had access to a private airstrip. That would work," Tess said. "We have to check if any of those could be in range."

She looked closely at Myra's face. None of the anguish of her final moments had marked her delicate features except for the bruising on her jaw and the cut on her lip. Tess closed her eyes and tried to visualize the assault. The heavy blow to her face that had left those marks. That blow must've made her dizzy and compliant, so the unsub found it easy to tie her hands behind her back with a cable tie. He came prepared . . . rapists always do. It used to be duct tape and rope, now it's cable ties. But how do you conduct such an assault on a plane? Where? There's no physical room, not enough space. Her arms and legs should carry bruises from being crushed against plane seats, even if in a private plane.

But why on a plane? Just because he could then fly them out and drop them in the water to never be found again? That was a good enough reason, but it sounded complicated and expensive at the same time.

So, he's rich. The cost of a few hours of jet time doesn't make him flinch.

But then again, how do you open the cabin door of a jet in flight, when you actually can't?

It's not how I would do it, Tess thought bitterly. *Raping her elsewhere and just hauling her to the plane makes more sense, but even so, it's risky as hell.*

She'd always been able to put herself in the killer's frame of mind and figure out his process. But this time, she failed to see why he'd choose such a complicated and risky location—an airport filled with potential witnesses and covered entrance-to-tarmac by dozens of video surveillance cameras. The worst possible place to lure a victim to be raped and killed.

Unless the plane meant something to him. Unless it was relevant to his psychopathology somehow.

Or unless the plane was part of his lure. Not many career-minded professionals would say no to a private jet ride with pretty much anybody. Their defenses would be dropped to zero because the private jets usually come with a pilot and a flight attendant. No reason to fear boarding one.

But none of that meant anything because a jet's door can't

be opened during flight. Period.

How about a transport plane? Military or cargo? That would answer all the questions about loading the body onto the plane and opening the door in mid-flight. Cargo planes do that. But who flies a cargo plane alone?

Still, the most agonizing question was a different one: had there been more victims?

"Doc, how fast do you estimate she hit the water?"

"I'd say close to terminal velocity, about one hundred miles per hour."

Michowsky whistled. "That kills my backup theory. I was thinking maybe someone lifted her up in one of those parasailing contraptions."

"Interesting thought," Tess admitted. "Doc, could that have worked? In that case, we're looking for a man with access to a fast boat equipped for parasailing, rather than a pilot with a plane."

"It could have if the line was long enough," he replied, now typing surprisingly quickly on his keyboard. "Says here that most parasailing lifts to five hundred feet, and a fall from that height won't reach the velocity I'm talking about. But a fall from a thousand feet would."

"Could she have fallen from way higher?" she asked. "Like ten thousand feet maybe?"

"She could have. I can't say definitively, because anywhere after one thousand feet, she would've reached terminal velocity and her speed would've remained constant at about one hundred miles per hour, maybe one twenty. She was thin, only one hundred and thirty-five pounds, and that puts her terminal velocity at about one hundred and thirteen miles per hour, but wind and currents might've had an impact."

"Did you notice any bruising that could've come from her body being slammed against plane seats or manipulated in a narrow space, like you'd expect on a small plane?"

He frowned, thinking for a moment, then he flipped quickly through the bluish images on the wall screen.

"Nothing conclusive. Most bruises can be explained by the assault she endured. These are where he pinned her down," he pointed at the screen in various places. "These are where he hit her, and those are strangulation marks. But there's no bruising or trauma of any significance on her back, her ribs, or her legs to support your scenario."

Damn it, she thought. *How the hell did he pull it off? And how was this MO relevant to him?*

"Doc," she asked, "One more question. What exactly happens with a body after falling into the Gulf of Mexico like hers did?"

He straightened his back and rubbed the root of his nose, where his glasses, after being worn for hours, had left deep indentations. "A body will initially sink, if the air can escape the lungs, and descend to the bottom of the water, where crabs and shrimp start doing their work, while putrefaction kicks in. After about three days, there will be enough accumulation of decomp gasses in the abdominal cavity to increase the body's buoyancy and resurface it. At this time, the skin has been softened enough by water to make it appealing for all kinds of fish. Even some sharks could take a bite, although normally they prefer live prey. And if a storm occurs, that body could soon disintegrate and be completely consumed by marine life."

"Could there have been others? Like Myra?"

He nodded with sadness. "I hate to say it, but yes, countless others, and we would've never been the wiser. This is the closest I've come to seeing a perfect murder, at least for the body disposal part of the crime. There's no evidence, no DNA, and, except this unique streak of luck, no body. What else is there?"

Tess stared at Myra's pale features, her long, dark chestnut hair settled in luscious waves around her head. "We still have Myra. She'll tell us her story."

5

MYRA

"What's on your mind?" Tess asked, seeing Michowsky's deep frown and white knuckles on the steering wheel.

They were headed to Myra's house to perform the most disturbing part of their job: the next-of-kin notification. She always felt a knot in her stomach in anticipation of delivering the message, knowing the devastation such news brings upon a family. She found herself feeling grateful that Myra's parents were both deceased. Far too many times, she'd told mothers their children weren't ever coming home.

"It's nothing," Michowsky said in a rushed, quiet voice, barely audible with all the noise from the rush-hour highway traffic.

"I would've assumed that after so many years of police work, you'd be a better liar," Tess replied. "Come on, spill it."

He pressed his lips together in a straight, tense line and shot Tess a quick glance, brimming with frustration. "It's my daughter," he eventually said, letting out a long, bitter sigh. "I believe she might be pregnant."

"Oh," Tess reacted. "I guess congratulations wouldn't be in order then?"

"She's seventeen, for Pete's sake," he replied angrily, delivering a blow to the steering wheel with the heel of his hand. "I didn't know she had a boyfriend. I didn't even know she was, um, sexually active." He cussed under his breath, then continued, his words bitter and harsh. "It's this damn job, taking every piece of soul we've got left in us. I'm too old for it, that's what's going on, if you really want to know. By the time I get home, I'm happy if I can walk straight and stand for long enough to take a shower."

"How old are you, partner?" she asked gently, but he didn't reply, keeping his eyes trained on the busy highway and his hands clenched on the wheel as if he was clinging to it for dear life.

He honked angrily at a driver who was distracted, texting with both his hands while doing seventy miles per hour. Then he flipped on the siren for a second and chuckled when the driver freaked and dropped the phone, then swerved out of the way.

"I should pull his ass over and rid him of that driver's license," he said. "These people with their damn phones, more lethal on the roads than anything else."

"And your damn age too," Tess said, her voice uncompromising now. "I'd really like to know when I should start saving for a nice flower arrangement for your funeral."

"Ahh, Winnett!"

"Yeah, it's me talking to you, while your self-pity party has no place in this vehicle." She allowed a few seconds to see if he was going to say anything, then continued. "So, what if she's pregnant? You're not ready to be a grandpa, is that it?"

"Look who's talking," Michowsky replied. "How many kids do you have?"

The unexpected blow silenced her. How was she supposed to explain that after what had happened to her twelve years ago, she wasn't able to let any man get close. Not until recently, but even that bit of blooming romance had scared her so badly she'd breathed with ease when Fradella was accepted into the Quantico FBI training academy. Michowsky's old partner was studying to become a federal agent, at a safe distance from Miami. She still didn't know if she wanted him to return or secretly hoped he'd get assigned elsewhere.

If he came back, would she be able to handle a normal relationship?

She swallowed with difficulty, her throat dry and raspy, constricted by the wave of unsettled emotions Michowsky's comment had brought to her mind.

"We deserve each other, don't we?" she asked weakly, feeling defeated.

"You didn't deserve that, and I'd kick myself if I weren't driving. When we get there, please slap me hard," Michowsky said. "I mean it."

"Nah . . . no need for violence in the workplace," she laughed quietly. "We have enough of that as it is."

They drove in silence for another few minutes, the drive through the sun-filled city seeming surreal against the backdrop of what they were set to do, against the vivid memory of Myra's frozen features on Doc Rizza's table, a memory Tess didn't seem to be able to shake.

She'd been someone's daughter.

"If your daughter's pregnant, she really needs you now, more than ever," Tess said. "Be there for her, that's all I want to say. Stay calm, whatever she decides to do, and yell at me if you really have to yell at someone. I'll be there for you."

"She's not even out of high school yet," Michowsky mumbled angrily, fueling his own fire.

"How do you know she's pregnant?"

"She throws up a lot, in the mornings," he replied. "She spends a lot of time in the bathroom, and I believe she's gained a little weight. And she's moody as hell."

Tess gave him a long stare. "This could be a million other things, partner. A moody teenager? Really? Who spends tons of time in the bathroom?"

"But she's barfing all the time," he pushed back. "What's up with that?"

"Why don't you ask her?" Seeing his clenched fists on the steering wheel, she added, "Or, better yet, have your wife ask her. She might be better suited to hear whatever is going on."

Michowsky pulled in at the address, a high-rise building on South Ocean Boulevard. Before he cut the engine, he turned to her and acknowledged with a nod.

"Myra lived with Stewart Aquilar, a scuba diving instructor," he clarified, checking his notes. "His DMV records show him at this address for the past two years. Myra owned the apartment."

"Let's hope we catch him before he leaves for work," Tess replied, checking the time with a quick frown.

Stewart Aquilar was home, and he answered the door in red swim trunks, his face partially covered in shaving cream and his hands wet. When he saw Tess's badge, he withdrew from the door as if he'd seen a monster, while color drained from his face, leaving it almost as white as the shaving cream.

"No . . ." he said, shaking his head in disbelief. He let himself drop against the wall until he reached the floor, his head hung low. "What happened?" he whispered. "Was it the plane?"

He wiped the foam off his face with his hands, then ran his palms against his trunks.

"What plane?" Tess replied, taken by surprise by his question.

He looked up at her with tear-filled eyes. "Did her plane crash?"

"No, Mr. Aquilar," she replied gently. "I'm sorry to say Myra was murdered."

He sprung to his feet, approaching Tess so quickly she pulled away. "What do you mean? Who killed her?"

"We're investigating her death," Michowsky intervened. "As soon as we know, we'll be in touch."

He shook his head again, this time more forcefully, pacing the living room as if looking for something to do to help him make sense of what was going on.

"We have some questions for you, Mr. Aquilar," Tess said.

"Anything," he replied, coming to a standstill and facing them.

"When did you notice she was missing?"

"I got worried last night when she didn't call," he replied, "When I got out of the water, I saw her missed call and message. I called her back, but we never connected. She was on a business trip in Houston and was supposed to get back late last night. I called her, left a couple of voicemails, but I assumed she'd had an overbooked flight or something. That happened a lot. But this morning, she still hadn't called, and I've been up since five, trying to figure out how to get in contact with her. I was going to go to her office, to ask if anyone knew anything."

"She worked at Southeast Chemical and—"

"Uh-huh."

"Who did she travel with?" Tess asked.

"When they do these platinum client presentations, it's her and her boss, Brad Galloway, maybe someone else from engineering. It was Brad for sure this time," he said, covering his mouth for a second to stifle a pained, shattered breath. "She hated traveling with him, and she'd bitched about it a lot before she left."

"When's the last time you spoke?" Michowsky asked.

"The day before yesterday, after the client demo. Myra was back at her hotel, happy the client had signed the contract. That meant a big commission for her."

"What time, exactly?"

"It was about nine-thirty P.M.," he said after a short hesitation. "Eight-thirty, Houston time. I can show you the time code on my phone."

Michowsky took the phone offered and started scrolling through the history.

"Was she going out anywhere?"

"Definitely not," he replied. "She was happy to be off her high heels. Those shoes were killing her feet. She was planning to order room service and call it a night."

"How about yesterday? What were her plans?"

"They were supposed to meet with the client in the morning for final arrangements, then lunch, then some shopping, if she managed to escape from Galloway, and then board the flight and come home."

"So, yesterday, you didn't speak with her at all?" Tess asked, frowning a little.

"We played telephone tag for a while, she called me and left a message, then I called her back and got her voicemail again. That's normal for us," he added with a shrug. "I'm in the water almost all day, and she's in meetings. And that boss of hers, Galloway, is a demanding asshole. He wants all of his employees' time, one hundred percent. He doesn't even allow restroom breaks when in meetings."

"Did you call him yet?" Tess asked.

Galloway seemed to be the closest thing they had to a lead so far.

"Not yet," Stewart replied, averting his gaze for a moment.

"Myra said she'd kill me if I called her boss or anyone else at her work. She didn't want me to embarrass her with 'my anxieties.' Her words, not mine," he added with a sad chuckle. "Life was hard for her at Southeast, a young and ambitious woman like her who wanted to make her own path in life."

Tess studied the young man. He seemed ready to collapse on the cold tiles but made an effort to maintain his composure and answer their questions. She'd considered him as a suspect for about a split second, then ruled him out. No one could fake that pallor, the dilated pupils from shock, fear of a life to be lived without a loved one, the almost unnoticeable tremors in the hands, the weakness in his knees. No . . . Stewart Aquilar had nothing to do with Myra's death.

"One more question, Mr. Aquilar. Do you know what hotel she was staying at?"

"Um, yes, a big, fancy one," he said, extending his hand to Michowsky to get his phone back. "She was thrilled that Galloway had paid for such a classy stay. That wasn't the norm with that cheap bastard." He flipped through his notes quickly. "She stayed at The Post Oak Hotel."

Tess thanked him and turned to leave, when Stewart touched her arm. Tears were running freely from his eyes now, while his chin trembled in a failed effort to contain his sobs.

"Please catch who did this to Myra," he pleaded. "We were going to get married in September. We were going to start a family, a big one, like neither of us had."

"I promise," Tess said, then shook his frozen hand before leaving. "I'm really sorry for your loss, Mr. Aquilar."

As soon as they reached Michowsky's SUV, she called the Houston hotel where Myra had stayed and spoke with the receptionist.

"Guess what?" Tess said, after ending the call with the hotel. "Myra left the hotel right before noon yesterday, alone, luggage and all, not showing any sign of distress. She was actually very happy, the receptionist remembers checking her out while she was smiling widely, excited about her stay, about the dinner she'd had, even though it was alone. The valet hailed a cab for her, and she was gone."

"Did you ask for the surveillance tapes?"

"They'll send the video of Myra getting in the cab," Tess confirmed.

"I wonder if she was really that alone," Michowsky replied. "Overnight, I mean. We should talk to her boss next."

"I've asked Donovan to pull Myra's phone records. No calls were made to and from her phone, to anyone but Stewart. Let's assume for now she was alone, but I'll follow up with hotel security. They should be able to send everything they have of Myra, including who entered her room. Maybe we'll get lucky."

They drove in silence for a moment.

Then Michowsky said, "I'm surprised you haven't profiled the perp yet."

6

ANGER

There had to be a way to break free of Geneva Wilkes.

There had to be, only Richard hadn't found it yet, not after four years of despicable slavery, of constant humiliation in public and behind closed doors.

In public, Geneva interrupted him, criticized every move he made or word he spoke, had him incessantly deliver her drinks and food, even dog treats for her mutt, although there were hordes of staff available to cater to her many whims. But no. Her impossible whims were reserved only for him. The rest of humankind was treated with elegance and respect by the steel heiress. While he, Richard Sanford, heir to a billion-dollar fortune, was to be ridiculed and laughed at by his wife's many girlfriends.

In private, Geneva's personal brand of torture exceeded his wildest imagination. Every few weeks, she came up with something new, a different form of humiliation, just to remind him she was in charge and she owned every part of him, body and soul, past, present, and future. Her latest demand still made his skin crawl when he remembered. She'd tied him up to "experience the pleasure of bondage himself," and because "otherwise he's too dangerous and cannot be trusted," and had forced him to perform oral sex on her until she was satisfied. Afterwards, she left him naked and tied up on the floor for hours, while she was in the next room, having coffee with her ever-present girlfriends and discussing his most intimate details without a shred of shame.

Oh, how he dreamed of the day he'd get his hands on his dear wife, to show her who he really was. Even that ill-fated, wine-infused night where he'd lost control with her, he'd managed to be moderate, gentle even by his own standards. After all, she was just fine the next day; not like she needed to see a doctor or anything. Maybe he should've just killed her then, when the bitch was tied up and her screams were smothered by her lacy, cream-colored La Perla panties shoved all the way in her damned mouth.

He'd never killed a woman before, but he wouldn't hesitate now. Not if he could get his hands on dear, old Gen. Or any of her girlfriends from hell.

He'd seen the way those women were staring at him whenever they ran into him at the mansion. They gave him these furtive looks, followed by whispers among themselves and poorly suppressed giggles at his expense, no doubt.

What he wouldn't do to the lot of them . . . one by one, or all at the same time.

Just thinking of that, just fantasizing of them screaming and begging for mercy, with Geneva served at the end like exquisite dessert, was sure to make him stiff and achy, his urges dire and merciless.

One such day, while he was still shaking with repressed rage, he'd run into his father in the downstairs living room.

Mr. Sanford senior, who had sold him into slavery like a seventeenth-century virgin. His father, who could've died by now and set him free, but instead clung to life and seemed to be thriving by Wilkes's side, now having found a best friend in his new business partner.

"Just the man I wanted to see," his father had greeted him jovially. "Come on, have a drink with me, son." He filled two glasses and handed one to Richard. He gulped it down, not even feeling the burn of the aged scotch on his parched throat.

"What can I do for you?" he asked, the lack of enthusiasm in his voice unconcealed.

"I've been hearing from Wilkes, you know. You need to keep that young wife of yours happy, son. A child might be in order, or two. Sanford Wilkes Enterprises needs an heir, and soon."

"I'm afraid my marriage is doomed," he said, determined to break free once and for all. "Geneva and I have nothing in common, and we're not happy. I will file for divor—"

"Nonsense," the old man bellowed. "You get that wife of yours pregnant, you hear me?"

"The merger will stand even if we divorce, Dad. I've seen the paperwork," he pleaded. "It's been years. If you want out of the merger, I'm sure some financial arrangement can be reached. Either we buy him off, or he buys us—"

His father's hand landed hard across his face, sending him off balance, seeing stars.

"How dare you?" the old man shouted. "You haven't built this company with *your* blood, *your* sweat, and *your* tears . . . I have! Before I hear you say another word, I'd just as soon put you in the ground myself. If the Sanfords aren't fit enough to lead this business into the future, maybe the Wilkes are."

Richard rubbed his cheek where it smarted, blinking away tears of frustration and staring at the old man in disbelief.

"Are you saying—"

"I'm saying this is your last warning, Richard. Make that nice wife of yours happy and pregnant while Wilkes and I can still show a grandson the ropes. Or else, I swear to God, I hear one more sigh from that woman or see Wilkes frown one more time when your name is spoken, and you won't inherit a single cent. I'll make sure no one will hire you, and no respectful bank will consider loaning you any money."

He stood there, unable to articulate a single word. How could he fight his old man, if his mind was already made up, if he'd fallen so badly under the Wilkes' family spell? If Wilkes was anything like his daughter, Richard didn't stand a chance against the two of them.

"What if I just leave the family business altogether?" he offered. "Would that make things better?"

"After I have built an empire, to die without a son? You call that better?" he shouted.

In the next room, one of the housekeepers rushed out and closed the doors behind her.

"I'd still be your son—"

"Make no mistake, if you walk out that door, if you choose to abandon me, you're no son of mine!"

Fueled by the slow-burning rage that had been consuming him for the past years, he found the courage to approach his father with newly found determination.

"There has to be something I can do about this. I won't stay married to her. I'm unhappy with—"

"Unhappy? Do you think I care about your unhappiness when my entire life's work is about to go into the ground? Everyone's buying from China these days, and we have to compete!" His voice had turned croaky and choked from the effort, and probably his blood pressure was spiking too.

Not high enough, damn him to hell, Richard thought.

He'd hidden his white-knuckled fists inside his pockets, fighting the urge to strike the life out of the old man and be done with everything once and for all. If his father were to die, he'd sell his share of the company to Wilkes or to the highest bidder of the moment, and disappear to some place where girls were easy and didn't complain much if they knew what was good for them.

He considered striking him dead, but then his courage withered; too many things could go wrong, and he could end up in jail. He bowed his head, defeated, while anger burned him raw. "As you wish. You'll have your grandson."

He didn't remember how he walked out of that room, if any other words were spoken, or how he got to Sanford Wilkes Enterprises. Just seeing the name, Wilkes, in brushed steel on the lobby wall made him want to tear it down with his bare hands and bellow his rage at the glass walls until they came tumbling down, like a modern-day Samson and the temple.

"Mr. Sanford?" A woman's excited voice brought him back to reality.

She was amazing, a dream in a white dress that hugged her slim waist and her voluptuous breasts. Her long, brown hair played hide-and-seek with her generous cleavage, while her smile promised a world of wonders, his to explore.

"Yes," he replied, smiling and shamelessly measuring her up.

"I'm Glenda Phelps, with Miami channel seven," she said, offering her hand.

He shook it a few moments longer than was customary, but she didn't withdraw or lower her gaze. Instead, her smile widened while she tilted her head to the side just a little. She batted her eyelashes a couple of times, and he swallowed hard.

"What can I do for you, Miss Phelps?" he asked.

"Please, call me Glenda," she asked, and he nodded. "I was wondering if we could spend some time together to go over some questions I have. We might do a piece on you, sometime in the next couple of weeks, if that's okay."

He looked at her for a long moment, weighing his decision. She wasn't someone who could easily be silenced, but neither were his desires . . . not anymore. First, he had to remove her from the eyes of so many witnesses.

"Sure, why don't we grab a cup of coffee in my office?"

He watched the sensuous movement of her hips while she walked, her legs long and taut on four-inch heels, her back straight and curving perfectly into a tight, inviting ass. And her hair . . . was just like Geneva's.

He pressed the penthouse button and smiled, while darkness descended in his eyes and lit his body on fire.

7

INTERVIEW

"It's a little too soon to deliver a profile," Tess admitted reluctantly, while Michowsky made his way through thick rush-hour traffic. Southeast Chemical and Paper was only a few miles away, but it was taking more than the ten minutes Tess had anticipated. A couple of car crashes on the interstate had them moving at snail speed, despite the flashing lights that did little to clear a path for the black Suburban.

"You must have some idea," Michowsky replied. "Anything could be helpful; you know that better than I do."

"How would it be helpful if I rush into a profile and I'm wrong?" Tess replied. "All I have is one victim, Myra. We don't even know that much about her and absolutely nothing about any other victims, other than the fact that I'm willing to bet my paycheck that they exist."

"Exactly," he said. "If they exist, who are they?"

She sighed; a long breath of air ended in a stifled groan. "No way of telling, M. They could be any woman who has crossed the unsub's path."

"What does that famous gut of yours tell you right now?" Michowsky insisted, after glancing quickly in her direction.

"All we really know is what he's done to her," Tess replied. "We don't know why he chose her or what Myra was to him. Was she someone who provoked him in any way, or so he thought in his diseased mind? Is she a substitute for the object of his anger? In this case, we'd expect the other victims to have some common physical features with Myra. Age, race, appearance."

She paused for a moment, looking absentmindedly at the driver in the next vehicle. The man was nervous to find himself so close to an unmarked law enforcement vehicle with its flashers on. Every few seconds, he glanced quickly toward them, as if hoping they'd miraculously vanish from the solid traffic jam.

"All I can say with a reasonable degree of certainty is that he's a power rapist. To him, it's about asserting power over his victims, and that's where he finds his sexual release. He carries a lot of unresolved anger, and he might feel powerless in his day-to-day existence, so powerless he feels the need to set things straight, to defend his identity, his ego, his masculinity by raping and killing his victims."

"He's not a lust killer then?"

"If I were to place a bet, I'd say he's motivated by power, not lust. Again, we don't have nearly enough to know for sure who we're dealing with. If we'd found a second victim, then I'd be more certain. But in lust killers, the torture and mutilation are key elements of the unsub's sexual fantasy. I didn't see mutilation or torture on Myra . . . just the traumatic evidence of a brutal and prolonged assault."

"Was her death a countermeasure? Could it have been?" Michowsky asked.

Tess mulled the question for a moment in her mind.

"Like with most power rapists, their first kill is an experimentation, maybe things being pushed too far, maybe the victim was killed to be silenced. Was Myra his first victim? I don't believe so. In my gut, I don't, although we have zero evidence one way or the other."

She paused again, replaying in her mind what she'd just

said. "To clarify, was Myra his first rape victim? Definitely not. He came equipped with cable ties, knew what to do, did it over and over without apparent inhibition or fear of getting caught. If he were a beginner at this game, the assault would've been shorter. He would've been satisfied sooner. What we've seen in the coroner's report and on Myra's body speaks to his experience as a rapist. As a killer? I'm not sure. I'd need to see at least another victim, and that's because of the specific cause of death. Is he so inexperienced at killing that he thought he'd killed her while strangling her? Or was the elaborate asphyxia and release just a power game, and she was meant to die hitting the water as part of an elaborate signature we don't yet understand? There's no way we can tell. Not right now."

"These sick bastards leave a trail of victims in their wake, they always do," Michowsky said. "Once we have an idea who this perp might be, we'll know."

"Exactly," she said. "And we'll catch him, I promise." She opened her laptop and switched through a few screens. "Bradley Galloway, fifty-one years old and Myra's 'favorite' boss by all accounts, has a clear record. He's single and has worked for Southeast for seven years. Let's see what he's got to say. He seems to be the last person to have seen Myra alive."

Michowsky pulled over at the main entrance of Southern Chemical and Paper and flashed his badge at the security guard who rushed to send the Suburban on its way to a parking spot.

They were escorted quickly into Galloway's office by a flustered and gossip-hungry assistant who did her best to uncover the reason why law enforcement was visiting her boss. When she opened the door to Galloway's office and showed them in, Tess saw a glint of amused excitement in her eyes. She'd probably paste her ear to the door as soon as she closed it.

Galloway stood abruptly as they walked in and barely glanced at the credentials Tess presented. He was an overweight and sweaty individual with a worried look on his face. He wore his tie too tight around his neck, which might've contributed to the congested aspect of his skin and his overall demeanor of panicked discomfort.

Or maybe their presence had that effect on Galloway.

He invited them to sit, and Tess obliged, noticing a laptop bag open under the man's desk. Inside, she could see a laptop, but there was a second laptop in use on his desk, among scattered paperwork and several pens bearing the company logo.

"What is this about?" he asked, clearing his voice before he could speak clearly.

Fear had that effect, to constrict the throat and dilate the pupils. One look at Galloway's eyes confirmed Tess's theory.

"We're looking into the disappearance of your employee, Myra Lambert," Tess replied.

"Disappearance?" Galloway reacted. "When she didn't show up for work this morning, I assumed she was jet-lagged, nothing more."

"You two were on a business trip together, right?" Michowsky asked.

"Yes," he admitted, his nervousness through the roof. He constantly rubbed his hands together, and his eyes moved from Tess to Michowsky and back, and then focused on various points in space, avoiding them altogether.

"Was there anyone else with you and Ms. Lambert?" Tess asked. "From Southeast, I mean."

"N—no, just us. Usually, we don't need engineering staff to

make a presentation and close a deal."

"When did you fly back from Houston?" Michowsky asked.

"Um, yesterday evening," he cleared his throat again and continued. "The flight landed at seven or so."

"And wasn't Ms. Lambert supposed to fly back with you?"

"She was . . . but I believe she missed her flight."

"She didn't show at the airport? That's what you're saying?" Tess asked.

Galloway was definitely hiding something. He was scared and elusive, but, at least so far, he wasn't lying.

"She didn't show, yes."

"Weren't you two supposed to share a cab from the hotel?"

He lowered his panicked gaze before replying. "She, um, didn't like traveling with me. I don't know why, but she even told me once she preferred to be by herself."

"Was she booked on the same return flight with you?" Tess asked.

"Yes," he replied reluctantly, after hesitating for a long moment.

"So, when she didn't show, what did you do?"

"I called her, but the call went to voicemail," he replied, touching his face briefly and shielding his eyes.

Tess didn't need to consult Myra's phone records to know he was lying. He hadn't called her.

"Are you sure about that, Mr. Galloway?" she asked calmly. "I have to remind you at this point that making a false statement to law enforcement is a felony."

"Ugh, sorry . . . I wanted to call her, but now I remember the flight attendant told me to turn off my phone." He wiped the sweat off his brow with his sleeve, leaving a wet stain on the blue fabric. "I assumed she decided to change her flight, that's all. I don't micromanage my employees. It's a free country."

"How did the presentation go?" Tess asked, changing direction abruptly. She noticed the tension in his shoulders dissipating a little. He swallowed and breathed a little easier.

"It went really well. I had my doubts, being it's such a big account, but we did our work really well to prepare for the presentation, and everyone showed up, so we were able to close the deal." Satisfaction seeped through his words, a bit of pride too.

"Who was it with?" Michowsky asked.

"With Sanford Wilkes," he replied without skipping a beat. "The company will buy its industrial packaging materials from us. It's a ten-year contract. We're hoping to add janitorial to that, for the entire enterprise."

Michowsky pushed a page torn from his notepad in front of Galloway. "We'll need the names of everyone who attended the presentation."

"Sure," he replied, sounding relieved. "Young Mr. Sanford was there, and all his top executives from finance, operations, and marketing," he listed, while scribbling names. He consulted the calendar on his laptop every now and then and kept writing. "Sanford's assistant was there too, and someone from the warehouse, and that's about it."

"Did anything unusual happen during the meeting?" Tess asked, frowning.

What was he afraid of? His reaction was paradoxical.

"No, not that I can think of," Galloway replied. "Sanford was a bit cold and rushed at first, but that's not unusual with the billionaire types. I was surprised he stayed through the entire thing. He had good questions though."

"Did anyone interact with Ms. Lambert more than others or

in an unusual way?"

He shook his head. "No. She did her thing, then I took all the questions and we sealed the deal. There was no dinner invitation for us, nothing like that. They're just too big to care. We're not a strategic vendor to them, but we hope to be."

The more corporate lingo the man spewed, the more confident he sounded. Tess needed him thrown off his game, and quickly.

"When was this presentation? Yesterday?"

"No, the day before," he replied, without skipping a beat.

"Why not return the night before? It's a short flight."

"We did the client engagement session yesterday morning. To save time."

"And?" Michowsky asked, while Tess leaned back against her chair, thinking, studying him closely.

Nothing out of the ordinary seemed to have happened during the business portion of the trip. Whatever he was hiding, it had nothing to do with that.

Galloway shrugged. "Just . . . nothing. An operational readiness assessment, to see how we will engage and when. The deal was signed the night before."

"Then what happened?" Tess asked. "Walk me through it, step by step."

No nervousness yet.

"Myra and I shared a cab to the hotel. We each went to our respective rooms. I checked out and left for the airport. The rest you know."

All his earlier anxiety was now gone.

"How about the night before? After signing the deal? Did you celebrate?" Michowsky asked.

"No. I invited Myra to join me for dinner, but she declined, saying she preferred to order room service and be on FaceTime with her boyfriend."

"And you didn't see her that night?" Michowsky pressed, but whatever had been there earlier to cause his anxiety was now gone.

"No. Not until we went to Sanford for the client engagement session yesterday morning."

"So, you have no idea where Ms. Lambert could be?" Michowsky asked.

"None whatsoever." He shrugged again; one shoulder rose slightly higher than the other.

Bingo.

"Tell me, Mr. Galloway. Why do you need two laptops?" Tess asked.

Color drained from his face, leaving it a sickly gray. His eyes dropped to the laptop bag at the foot of his desk. Whatever he had to hide was on that laptop and could hold the key to catching Myra's killer.

"This? It's easier for me," he croaked, his throat constricted again. He cleared it and continued. "When I travel, I mean."

"Could I take a look?" Tess asked, extending her hand and waiting, noticing how new drops of sweat popped at the roots of his hair.

He tugged at the knot of his tie, releasing it a good two inches. "Um, don't you need a warrant for that?"

Tess withdrew her hand. "Sure. We'll get one right away. Until I'm back with the warrant, my colleague, Detective Michowsky, will keep you company to make sure no evidence is removed from either laptop."

She stood, getting ready to leave. Michowsky's eyes met hers in silent agreement, while Galloway tugged at his tie some more.

He sprung from his chair, agitated. "How about me?" he asked, his voice a higher pitch. "Am I supposed to sit here and just wait?"

"We could place you under arrest instead, if you prefer," Michowsky offered.

He backed away abruptly, panicked. "No . . . please, don't. I don't know anything, I swear."

Tess nodded to Michowsky. She'd seen enough.

The detective took out a pair of cuffs and grabbed Galloway's arm, twisting it behind his back.

"You're under arrest for the murder of Myra Lambert. You have the right—"

"Wait, murder?" he shouted. "Myra's dead?"

8

MILE HIGH

Glenda wiped the blood dripping from her mouth as soon as he untied her hands. Breathing heavily and still sniffling, her tears flowing freely down her cheeks, she sat on the edge of the bed with difficulty, then stood hesitantly, holding on to the handle built into the headboard. Where she'd sat, she left a blood stain on the white leather he'd have to wipe clean before his ground crew boarded the plane.

Damn it.

Richard was a little disappointed.

Glenda had shown lots of potential, seeming full of gumption and promising a fierce fight, but instead, she'd screamed until she'd run out of air, then started whimpering and sat still, letting him do anything he wanted to her, but it was like taking a warm corpse, not a living being. Despite his release, he was still tormented, yearning for the exhilaration he felt after subduing a beautiful creature who'd rather die fighting than be possessed by him.

But not this one. For the most part, she'd just lain there, delivering a deflating concert of wails and sobs that had almost withered him to the point of killing his libido completely.

Bummer.

Now he had all that bloody mess to clean up from the reclined bed, a couple of the seats, and the carpet in countless places, and who knows how much her silence was going to cost him.

In retrospect, taking a member of the fourth estate on the

flight might've been a terrible idea. What if he paid her off and she decided to talk after all? And what on earth possessed him to take her on the plane? Why not take her to a no-tell motel like he'd done with the rest of them, a place anonymous and discreet, from where he could disappear without a trace.

The plane complicated things.

His intentions had been to impress her, to woo her even. His public image needed some professional help, and she'd seemed like the right person for it. But seeing her aboard his jet, vulnerable, available, and willing had pushed all his buttons. He'd set the autopilot on and took her to the back.

That's where he lost control, the control he'd promised himself he wouldn't lose with her, no matter what. Now he had bloodstains to clean and a potential disaster waiting to happen, by the name of Glenda Phelps.

He looked at her and found her wearing her torn dress, shoes in hand, looking disheveled, lost. She had nowhere to go, that was the immense beauty of his Gulfstream G650ER. He loved that plane and was thrilled with the possibilities the bedroom in the aft compartment opened for him. Maybe Glenda wouldn't be the last guest to be shown the extended tour of the jet. It had cost him a fortune to have that section built, but it was worth every dime of his tax write-off.

"I—I won't tell a soul," she whimpered, "just please, let me go."

He laughed, a quick, cruel cackle. "Am I to assume our interview has been canceled?"

He stood and walked to the cockpit, still naked, enjoying the aircraft's powerful ventilation on his heated body.

"We'll still do the interview," she rushed to reassure him. "I'll say whatever you want me to say."

He weighed his options for a long moment. He imagined her deplaning upon arrival, blood still trickling on the inside of her leg, dress torn at the cleavage, her lip swollen, her left eye almost completely shut. No way he could have his ground crew see her like that.

The plane was great for his flavor of sex, but motels had benefits. No way he could just up and go now. He had to deal with this mess.

But maybe there was a way. Maybe he could land at a different airport, a small one preferably, so she'd hail a cab and go home without being seen.

He opened an overhead compartment where his flight attendant kept her work clothes and extracted a few items.

"Put these on," he said, throwing the blouse and skirt at Glenda's feet. "Wipe yourself clean, and put your shoes on."

She rushed to obey him, stifling her sobs.

He sat in the pilot's seat and looked at the maps. He'd flown far over the Gulf of Mexico. It would take him another hour to get above land. A little research found a smaller airport outside of the crowded areas of South Florida. He set the new destination and let the autopilot take over the flying. Then he went in the cabin, where he found Glenda dressed in new, clean clothes, attempting to smile through tears.

"How much do you want?" he asked without any introduction. His voice was cold, businesslike, matter-of-fact. He'd done this part so many times in the past, it felt like routine for him.

"What do you mean?" she asked quietly, glancing at him for a split second, then looking away.

"To keep quiet about the best sex you've ever had," he replied, laughing again. "So, how much?"

Her whimpers stopped. They always stopped crying at that particular point in the conversation. Apparently, one cannot cry and think numbers at the same time.

"I'll give you time to think until we land," he said, then went back to the cockpit. "Get in here," he ordered, "I need you seated and strapped in for the landing."

He was still naked, the promise of a new erection touching his senses when he saw her wince as she took her seat. She'd remember him for a while, that was a guarantee.

"If I drop you off at Pahokee Airport. Will you be okay from there?" he asked, retaking the controls and preparing for descent. "Anyone hears about our little escapade and the deal is off."

"Uh-huh," she replied, nodding.

"There will be an NDA to sign, later today, and the payment will be cash," he added, sounding almost courteous, much to his own surprise.

There was no tower to contact at this airport, so he lined up with the runway and adjusted his speed. He extended the flaps and deployed the landing gear, then glanced at Glenda.

The look he saw in her eyes stunned him to the point of almost botching the landing. It was as if Geneva had come to possess Glenda's body. Her eyes were dry and cold, her swollen lips tight, her attitude completely metamorphosed into something he recognized too well.

"I think I know what I want," she said dryly as he made the final approach. "This plane would be nice, for starters. And about four million a year, for the rest of your life. If I need more money to operate it, be kind and let me know what to ask for."

"Huh," he reacted, his eyes riveted to the cockpit controls. "Not going to happen. You might've been reasonably compliant back there and a decent fuck, but you sure as hell ain't worth that much."

"Then your pretty, little, rich wife will kick you to the curb for the mile-high roll we just did here. Entirely your call. Unless you'd prefer to go to jail for rape?"

The stall warning came on, an indication that the touchdown speed had been reached.

In a split second, his decision was made. Just as his wheels were touching the runway, he gave the roaring engines gas, pushing the thrust levers all the way up and lifting the nose.

As soon as he could take his hand off the controls, he slapped Glenda into silent compliance, then set the autopilot.

He unbuckled his seatbelt and stood, then grabbed her by the hair.

"No, please, no," she whimpered. "Forget I said anything," she pleaded.

"What kind of stupid do you think I am?" he shouted, dragging her toward the back of the plane, unsure what he was going to do with her. All he knew was that he wanted her silenced.

Forever.

"You're not a killer," Glenda said. "You like rough sex, and that's no crime. Please, let me go. Please," she wailed, letting herself drop to the floor as soon as he let go of her hair.

"How the hell do you know what I am?" he said, feeling waves of rage ripping through his body. Looking at Glenda, he so desperately wished it was Geneva sobbing and pleading at his feet, that he thought he saw his wife's uncompromising, steel-blue eyes looking up at him through a veil of tears.

"Please," she cried again. "Just let me go. I'll do anything you want." As she said the words, she collapsed to the floor, her shoulders heaving with every shattered breath she took.

Something must've changed in his eyes as he decided what to do with her, because she panicked and started hitting him, her arms flailing, her body thrashing desperately to get free of him.

"They know where I am," she said, spewing the words quickly and out of breath. "My editor knows. He'll tell the cops."

He slapped her across the face, his senses awakened by her resistance. Maybe there was still time to erase the earlier disappointment. He grabbed her arm and dragged her toward the back of the plane, while she screamed and kicked and clawed.

"You're a lame piece of shit," she yelled, staring him in the eyes with dilated pupils filled with rage. "An impotent who needs a plane to rape a woman, a no-good piece of worthless excuse for a human being. I hope you fry for this." All her fear was gone, and what was left behind he easily recognized.

Geneva.

In a trance, he put his hands around her neck and squeezed, tighter and tighter, until she stopped thrashing.

Breathing heavily, he let her body fall to the floor and closed his eyes, taking in the intense exhilaration. What a rush, what a transforming experience!

Before he opened his eyes moments later, he knew he was addicted. He knew he'd have to do this again and again.

Then he looked at the body lying at his feet and panic prickled the roots of his hair.

How could he get rid of the body?

He rushed to the cockpit and stared at the Garmin screen. The plane was over the Gulf again, well outside the range of shore radars. If he threw her body in the Gulf, no one would ever find her.

There was only one problem. He was an experienced pilot and knew he couldn't open the cabin door because of the immense pressure— at least not under the current flight parameters.

He sat in the pilot's seat and made adjustments. He started a descent to 800 feet and reduced airspeed to a few knots above stall. Then he turned off the cabin pressure and swallowed a few times to relieve the pressure he felt in his ears. He set the aircraft on a holding pattern above the green-blue waters of the Gulf and went back to the cabin.

It took all his strength to push open the Gulfstream's door. He dragged Glenda's body to the threshold and waited until the plane executed a left turn, banking, so that her body wouldn't hit the steps on its way down. He watched her body fall and hit the water with a splash that quickly disappeared, swallowed by the deep waters. He threw out all her clothes, her purse, and her phone, then he stood for a few long moments in the doorway, naked and erect, savoring the warm air as it brushed against his adrenaline-filled body.

Ninety minutes later, when he landed at his home base airport in Miami, all the ground crew noticed that was out of the ordinary was a tiny hint of a smile on his lips.

"How was your flight, sir?" the mechanic asked.

That unusual smile stretched his lips a little more. He took a photo of the plane with his phone camera, then replied, "Unforgettable."

9

SUSPECT

Tess studied Brad Galloway through the one-way mirror. He'd been stewing by himself in the interview room for about an hour, the time the technician needed to crack open his laptop and get an idea of what he was hiding. Now they knew.

Michowsky had stepped out to make a call and quickly returned with a beaming smile on his face.

"What's up, M? Did you solve the case all by yourself?"

"See for yourself," he replied, showing her his phone.

The message displayed was from his wife, and it read, "Not pregnant. Taking diet pills."

"Ah," Tess reacted. "So, you're really not ready to be a grandpa, are you?" she asked, laughing. "You still got time, don't worry."

He frowned at her, half-jokingly. "I'm not worried, believe me."

"Then let's deal with this piece of human refuse," she said coldly and entered the interview room.

Galloway looked disheveled and at the end of his wits. He was pale and sweaty, despite the chill coming from the air conditioning vents above his head.

"Finally," he said, springing to his feet the moment they came through the door.

"Sit down," Michowsky ordered.

He obeyed without another word, his mouth ajar and his eyes widened in fear.

"I swear I had no idea Myra was dead," he eventually said,

while Tess took her time to review the file she'd brought along, stretching his nerves a little more.

"Let's say I believe that," Tess replied. "That doesn't make you a law-abiding citizen, now, does it?"

He averted his eyes, staring at his feet for a moment. "I didn't do anything to Myra, and I don't know who did. You have to believe me."

This second statement didn't sound as truthful as his first words, not to Winnett's experienced ear. He was telling the truth about not having known Myra was dead, but when it came to him having no idea what had happened to the young woman, there was a hint of deception in his voice that she couldn't place. It wasn't full-blown guilt, like she'd notice if he'd been personally involved in her disappearance or had witnessed something of any relevance. No, it was more subtle than that, yet relevant and important, because he lied about it every chance he got.

Tess looked at Michowsky and he took over.

"At this point in time," he said, "I have to ask you if you have any statement to make that would help you with your situation," Michowsky said.

"What situation?" Galloway replied.

"Listen," Michowsky continued, lowering his voice as if to keep their discussion confidential from any potential observers from outside the room. "I was assigned to solve a murder, and I don't really care about other, um, indiscretions."

He looked at Galloway as he was speaking, noticing the impact his words had on the man. He was close to gaining his trust.

"It's hard when you're all alone, with a demanding job like yours, to stay on the straight and narrow all the damn time, right?" Michowsky asked, winking discreetly at Galloway.

The man nodded. "Yeah," he whispered, shooting a fearful glance at Tess, who pretended to be immersed in reviewing his file. "You know how it is," he added. "Sometimes you just can't help yourself."

"So, never mind that, maybe we can make it go away, especially if we wrap things up here before Technical Services has a chance to examine your laptop, that is. Let's stay focused on Myra."

"Yes," he offered quickly, almost excitedly. "What do you need to know?"

"Start from the beginning of the Sanford Wilkes presentation, and walk me through everything, again. Focus on what you might've left out earlier. Did anyone speak with Myra?"

"N—no," he replied, his voice carrying hints of the same fear and deception. "Myra did her thing, and then we were gone, after I took all the questions from the client."

"Tell me, Mr. Galloway," Tess intervened. "Since Sanford Wilkes is headquartered here, in Miami, why fly to Houston to do this presentation?"

"That's how the client wanted it," he replied quickly, sounding almost relieved. "The distribution center is in Houston, and the client wanted us to meet with some of the local executives."

"You said the client had questions, right?" Tess asked. "After the presentation?"

"Yes, quite a few," Galloway replied, the hint of a frown appearing on his forehead.

She was getting closer to whatever the man was hiding. Now, she had to patiently peel the onion and carefully watch his body language, the behavioral analyst's version of the hot and cold game that children play.

"Give me some examples of such questions," she asked.

Galloway clasped his hands together, probably to hide the slight tremor in his fingers.

"Um, their operations wanted to know how often we ship product, and if we're willing to abide by their just-in-time schedules. The VP of finance wanted to know if we would accept payment at ninety days, that kind of stuff. All pretty normal."

Cold again.

"How about any casual, friendly, or personal interactions you might have observed around Myra?" she asked.

He fidgeted in his seat and quickly ran his hand to the back of his neck, then clasped his hands together again.

Warmer.

"Nothing that I can think of," he replied. "Maybe there was something, but I don't remember."

Tess sprung to her feet and slammed the folder against the metallic table, startling Galloway.

"Mr. Galloway, we found child porn on your laptop, and that's a federal offense with a ten-year prison sentence. So, if there was ever a time for you to remember, that time is now."

Blood drained from his face, leaving him shaking, his entire body trembling badly, as if he were about to come apart at the seams.

"There was nothing, really, I—I s—swear," he stuttered. "We overheard Sanford order three dozen roses for his wedding anniversary, with a note to his wife. Then he seemed distracted during the meeting, so distracted I didn't expect him to last the entire hour."

He stopped talking, shielding his eyes from Tess's scrutiny.

"What else?" Michowsky demanded impatiently.

"Then he signed the contract right there, which almost never happens. I was happy, of course."

"Walk us through it," Tess asked, after exchanging a quick glance with Michowsky.

"When the questions were done, Sanford said something like, 'Okay, let's get this done already. Where do I sign?'"

"That's it?"

He hesitated for a short moment. "Yes, I believe so."

"Think harder," Tess whispered in his ear. "Your life depends on it."

"Usually, the lawyers take it to the next step and pore over contract details until both parties are satisfied," he explained. "I've never seen a multimillion-dollar contract signed on the spot like that."

"But that's not it, am I right?" Tess pushed. "What happened after the contract was signed?"

"Nothing," he said, a little too quickly.

All Tess had to do was scowl at him.

"Sanford asked where we were staying," he blurted. "I remember thinking it was a good thing we reserved rooms in a good hotel, so we'd make a solid impression. Then I was expecting a dinner invitation to come, which is very common when big contracts are signed and relationships are being built, but that invite never came."

Tess glanced quickly at Michowsky. Maybe the dinner invite hadn't come for Galloway, but it had for Myra. Young Mr. Sanford was their only lead into Myra's death, albeit very thin, almost invisible.

"Had Myra and Sanford met before the presentation?"

Michowsky asked.

"No, they were introduced in my presence."

"How did Sanford react to the introduction?" Tess asked.

"He was cold and distant, distracted. I already told you. He didn't behave like he wanted to be there. That's why I was so surprised when he decided to sign the deal."

"What did he do after signing it? Sanford, I mean?" Michowsky asked.

"Said thanks and disappeared."

"He didn't linger, didn't speak with Myra?"

"No," Galloway replied calmly. "He almost rushed out of there. Five minutes later, I saw him leaving the office in his Porsche."

Cold again. Icy cold.

"Mr. Galloway, this is the last chance I will give you," Tess stated formally. "What are you hiding?"

He lowered his gaze and shook his head slowly. "It might be nothing," he said bitterly. "Last thing I want to do is cast suspicion on a good client or jeopardize a deal like that."

"Out with it already," Tess demanded.

"There were rumors in the hotel that someone had closed an entire section of the most expensive restaurant on premises for one woman, who dined there alone, a young and beautiful brunette. I don't know who that was, I swear."

This time, his voice rang true.

"When we met for the client presentation the next day, I asked Myra about it, and she said she didn't know what I was talking about. So, I guess it was someone else, not her."

Tess and Michowsky exchanged a long glance.

It was time to go back to where it all started, The Post Oak Hotel in Houston. Just like Galloway, the hotel staff seemed to have some answers, but just like the sleazy piece of scum in front of them, they withheld information to protect the lining of their pockets.

"What's going to happen to me now?" Galloway asked, jumping to his feet as soon as Tess opened the door. "Can I go home now? I told you everything I know."

"You mean to tell me you lived to the ripe age of fifty-one years and you don't know what happens to pedophiles in our justice system?" Michowsky replied.

Galloway fell back on his metallic chair, his mouth agape. "But you said—"

10

MEETING

Richard found it difficult to focus these days, especially when he was trapped in endless meetings about one boring aspect of the business or another. The best he could do was pretend to be preoccupied by something important or stare at a stack of papers, letting his mind wander. Because rich, powerful people like him were never distracted or daydreaming; they were preoccupied.

Whatever it was called, he welcomed the escape from the grinding routine of the life he hated, savoring the moments of blissful reminiscence as he remembered the girls he'd taken up in the sky.

To him, *taken* meant so much more. He'd taken those girls in every possible way, taken ownership of their bodies, then taken their lives. He was the last thing they saw, his was the last name they screamed. And they'd all been wonderful.

His mind wandered into the past, thinking about Glenda.

She would always remain his first, none other able to kindle a fire in his groin like the memory of her.

Others had followed after Glenda, all memorable in their unique ways, their names forever carved in the darkest recesses of his mind. But his first would always be more special than all the rest.

After Glenda, he'd waited almost an entire year until he had the courage to invite another girl for a plane ride, afraid that one day the cops would bang on his door and his life, albeit beyond miserable as an eternal slave to his viciously vengeful wife, would end in a fate worse than his wildest nightmares. But days passed and, while the cops never showed, his old urges surfaced, more and more demanding with each day.

Every time he wondered if the new girl could recreate or exceed the intensity of the thrill he'd felt when Glenda's life was extinguished in his hands. Yet somehow, they all fell short of delivering the exhilaration he was looking for. Like a veritable addict, he needed bigger and bigger doses of the drug to get high, and the high he reached was never really high enough. Constantly yearning for something he couldn't reach and never fully satisfied, he kept trying.

Just as a spiraling addict, he needed his fix more and more often, willing to take any risk to get another jolt of that incredible feeling. He made mistakes and he knew it; unwilling to acknowledge the need for change, he kept on going. But he'd become smarter at how he did things, isolating himself from the girls who would soon be reported missing.

He'd recruited a young, male prostitute he found on the streets of the San Francisco Tenderloin, a man who'd readily kill for him with no questions asked. He found a kindred spirit in Michel, short for Michelangelo, the name his Italian mother had cursed him with. He was the one who'd deal with the girls, deliver his messages, and, if ever needed, assist with anything he needed. Michel was perfect for the job; he'd never been on the grid. He'd never had a driver's license, yet he moved through the world effectively and completely unseen, like a ghost. With Michel by his side, Richard had much better odds of never being caught.

He wasn't afraid; he'd never been afraid in his life, only prepared. And he definitely didn't want to stop.

Every woman he met, he evaluated instantly, deciding

whether he wanted to take her or not. If he didn't, the woman would never realize how lucky she'd been. If yes, he'd immediately start making plans, arranging things so that when his invitation would come, she could only accept.

His evaluation criteria remained the same, a strong resemblance to Geneva would be an instant qualifier for the girl who would soon have her life taken without beginning to understand why. A gratifying rehearsal after another, all in the hope that someday, when things would be just right, he could get the bitch from hell aboard his plane for a final, masterful fix that would make the earth move like never before.

One day he'd ask Geneva to fly to Houston, or someplace else with him. One day soon.

It was about bloody time.

He'd been married to her for ten endless years, celebrated without joy only two days before with an excruciating family function that brought the Sanford and Wilkes clans together for hours of mindless chatter and political plays.

Ten long years.

All this time, waiting for the opportunity to break free, making plans that never turned to reality, and squirrelling away cash in decent quantities to have, if his proclivities ever caught up with him and he needed to make a quick exit.

Since Glenda, he'd pushed himself to be the best husband possible, willing to take his wife's wrath but taking it with dignity and a little humor, slowly eroding her distrust and dissolving her anger. Just because he'd seen what it felt like to have someone's life end at his will, just because it pleased him. In a way, he'd killed Geneva over and over, his fantasies so real he was sometimes startled when he ran into her in the living room of his huge mansion.

It didn't matter that Geneva had given him a son, or so everyone thought. Little did they know that the boy came into existence as a coldhearted plan conceived by the two warring spouses. Richard, pushed by his father's demand for a son, took the request to Geneva as coldly as a business proposition, knowing exceedingly well he had no chance to land in her bed ever again. His wife, after the shouting match triggered by his request, took the matter into her own hands. He was promptly invited to make deposits at an in vitro clinic, whose chief doctor used them, in theory at least, to impregnate his wife. Seeing how the boy's hair was a reddish blond, reminding him more of his wife's doctor than of his own physiognomy, Richard never grew close to the boy. He'd never challenged him either, knowing that while Geneva was still alive, little could be done about the bastard living in his house.

Soon enough, none of that would matter. After Geneva would mysteriously disappear while he had an unbeatable alibi, he could request a DNA test for the child and oust him as the bastard that he was. That would probably kill his father on the spot, but that was nothing if not added incentive.

His plan had many moving parts and had to be executed with precision. But all he could do while he waited for the right moment was obsess over it, because thinking about only one thing the entire time could be called nothing else. He saw himself taking off with that vile, blood-sucking bitch onboard, and as soon as the autopilot was set, he'd join her in the cabin. At that point, she'd still believe there was a pilot onboard, that they weren't alone, and she'd be relaxed, selfishly absorbed by some magazine, not dignifying him with one look.

Then he'd walk over to her and grab a fistful of her hair with a quick gesture. She'd scream and—

"Mr. Sanford?" a voice interrupted his chain of thought, bringing him back to the present.

Frustrated to the point of cursing out loud, he snapped. "What?"

"Would you like to see anything else, sir?" the man asked, standing in front of a huge screen, looking like a pot-bellied idiot with that laser pointer in his hand.

Forcefully dragged back to reality, he realized he was still in a meeting. The screen displayed one slide bearing the vendor's logo and the word, "Questions?" in a black font. Helpful as fuck.

He frowned, trying to remember what the meeting was about. Instead, his eyes found the presenter's assistant seated across the glass table, smiling pleasantly with impeccable white teeth. Her visitor access pass had her name in block letters: Brittany.

Well, hello Brittany.

He pretended to check something in his printed materials but used the opportunity to study the woman's long legs, the fine tattoo that resembled a chain wrapped around her left ankle, the way her feet arched in her high-heeled sandals, her perfectly pedicured toes.

Then he looked at her smiling face again, at her perfect skin surrounded by shiny, chestnut waves of long, luscious hair. His demons yanked him away from reality again, as he imagined his fingers running through those sleek strands and twisting them tightly, until she couldn't move her head anymore, until she dropped powerless at his feet.

"I believe I've seen enough," he said calmly. "We're ready to proceed."

He stood, and the rest of those in attendance happily followed suit. The meeting was adjourned, and everyone's good spirits filled the room with small talk and laughter.

Filled with anticipation anxiety, he shook the presenter's hand, asking casually, "So, where are you guys staying?"

"At the Astoria," the man replied, smiling widely.

He searched the woman's eyes and found them eager, inviting.

11

RICHARD

"How would you like to have the entire Houston regional bureau deploy on premises to assist with our investigation?" Tess shouted at the SUV's media system. On the other end of the airwaves was the head of security of The Oak Post Hotel, the man responsible for withheld information, delayed surveillance videos, and vague answers, and that was just for starters. The hotel staff had been soft-blocking their investigation the whole time, a practical demonstration of passive-aggressive behavior.

Michowsky was weaving through lighter traffic on the way to Sanford Wilkes Enterprises, but Tess wanted to have a few more answers before interviewing a man who'd probably lawyer up before they finished walking through the door.

Only static came through the media center's speakers.

"Mr. Hawkins," Tess said, "let me make it very clear. Either you deliver all the answers we're looking for, or the Houston FBI will be at your door in twenty minutes to get those answers. What will it be?"

"Okay, Agent Winnett, what do you need to know?" Hawkins's voice sounded resigned, his pitch low and muffled, almost a whisper. He was probably breaking hotel procedure by cooperating with her without a warrant.

"I need to know everything Myra Lambert did in the twenty-four hours before her death, and she spent most of that time in your hotel."

The sound of rustling papers, then Hawkins's voice again.

"She checked out at eleven forty-five A.M., then took a cab. We have the cab's number from our video surveillance; I've already sent that to the detective."

Tess glanced at Michowsky, who nodded.

"Did anyone visit her room?"

"No," Hawkins replied. "My people checked every minute of surveillance on that floor. She had no visitors, and no calls were logged on the room landline."

"What about this mysterious dinner we heard about?"

Silence dropped heavy, amplifying the static on the line.

"Yes, there was a private dinner for which an entire section of the restaurant was reserved."

"Who ate there?" Tess asked, a little irritated she had to extract information from Hawkins with such difficulty.

"We believe it could've been Myra Lambert."

"You believe?" Tess mocked him. "You're not sure?"

"We only have cameras in the ceiling at the steakhouse, and there's an entire section of hallway that's not covered. So, yes, it could've been her. Similar hair, same dress color, not much else is visible in the restaurant, but after the dinner guest left the premises, we have Ms. Lambert returning to her hotel room a few minutes later. It's a strong possibility it was her."

"Did you show the waitstaff her photo to make sure?"

"We did not," he replied cautiously. "Our mandate is different here; I hope you understand. We serve our clients and their needs, not anyone else."

"Who paid for this fancy dinner?"

Tess thought she heard the man sigh.

"We don't know, Agent Winnett, I'm sorry."

"How can you not know?" she blurted, frustrated with the distance, with the impossibility of doing the legwork herself.

It was like trying to grasp at a glass window . . . nothing stuck.

"The deal was paid for in cash with very specific instructions. The client wasn't someone we've seen before."

"I'll need a photo of this client," she requested, then paused for a moment, thinking. "Mr. Hawkins, I believe there's a reason why you're being elusive with me, and I hope you don't cross the line to where I can slap an obstruction of justice charge on you. It's not something I want to do, but I will if I have to."

"We respect the privacy of our clients," he replied quickly. "And we gladly cooperate with law enforcement. After all, Ms. Lambert was our client, and we have a vested interest in catching her killer and bringing him to justice."

"Yeah . . . I bet you do," Tess replied, then ended the call.

"Anonymous dinner reservations, paid for in cash?" Michowsky asked as soon as the call ended, then honked at a careless driver who'd cut into his lane. "Who does that?"

"Someone who's covering his tracks and plans well ahead of time."

A chime warned Tess she had a new message, and before she could read it, a second chime was heard. The first message was the photo of the man who'd booked the restaurant. A grainy, low resolution image showed him carrying a silver briefcase, probably filled with cash. Tess had hoped it would be Richard Sanford, but this was a younger man. Thin, dressed in jeans, a hoodie, and a ballcap, and wearing sunglasses indoors. The surveillance shot wasn't worth much; the mysterious man had made sure of that. Even Donovan's top-notch facial recognition software would fail to identify him; only a small section of his face was visible.

The second text message was yet another blow to their investigation. Donovan had tracked down the cabbie who transported Myra Lambert from the hotel, but he was in the Intensive Care Unit at Houston Methodist, hooked on life support and not expected to recover. He'd suffered a massive stroke the night before.

"Sheesh," Michowsky said, after Tess delivered both messages. "We're not catching any breaks, are we?"

"Maybe we will catch one now," she replied, looking thoughtfully at the tall building that bore the Sanford Wilkes logo.

Moments later, they were invited into Richard Sanford's office. It was large and well lit, with floor-to-ceiling windows that faced the Atlantic Ocean, letting the sunshine in. Lushly decorated with modern art and furniture, with mahogany accents and LED lighting, it was a setting that belonged on the pages of architecture and design magazines. But the one piece of décor that caught Tess's attention was a series of eighteen photos of the same jet, the logoed company Gulfstream, taken at different times of day and in different locations, all from the tarmac. The images were neatly framed and arranged on the wall in two rows, one row of ten images, the second row of only eight images, as if incomplete.

She touched Michowsky's sleeve in passing as she approached the photos, to draw his attention, then studied them for a moment, although Sanford was waiting, standing impatiently behind his desk.

"What can I do for you, Agent, um, Winnett?" Sanford asked, a hint of irritation in his voice. "I have a meeting in about ten minutes."

She turned to face him and scrutinized his strong, masculine features, looking for signs of emotion, of fear. There weren't any. A slight furrow in his brow, maybe because they'd imposed on his busy day.

"I'm not sure if you're aware, but Myra Lambert, the Southeast Chemical and Paper project manager you met three days ago, has been found dead. Murdered."

"Oh," he reacted, his frown deepening as he shoved his hands in his pockets. He walked toward them, closing about half the distance. "I had no idea. I'm very sorry to hear that. What happened?"

"We're still investigating," Tess replied coldly. "But you were one of the last people to see Ms. Lambert alive. What can you tell us about the meeting you were in with the Southeast team?"

She continued to study his face, now closer, a little intrigued with the total lack of emotional response to the news she had delivered. With most people, news of someone's death triggers an emotion of sorts, an empathic response, a reaction to being reminded of one's mortality. But not with Richard Sanford; his face remained the same, relaxed, a little impatient, completely detached, uncaring.

She'd seen this type of behavior a few times before, but only in true psychopaths. Their minds don't carry the burden of fear or empathy and can remain calm, lucid, and focused under the direst circumstances.

He maintained casual eye contact, not trying too hard, not averting his eyes either. When he replied, his voice was steady and matter-of-fact.

"The meetings were quick and to the point, and we signed the deal. I don't particularly remember Ms. Lambert and can't recall if I spoke to her or not. I do a lot of these engagements, I'm afraid. After a while, they all blend together."

"I can relate," Tess replied, feigning sympathetic

understanding. "Anything you can recall would be greatly appreciated."

"Well, that's about it," he added with a shrug. "I flew back home that day and haven't spoken with Ms. Lambert or any other Southeast people since. My assistant handles any correspondence they might've sent."

"When did you leave Houston, Mr. Sanford?"

"Right after the onboarding session with the vendor. I like to pack in my meetings in the early morning, so I can handle the urgent business of the day in both locations. It's a short flight."

"Do you remember what time it was when you flew back?" Michowsky asked.

"I was at the airport by nine forty-five and took off right away, so I'd say ten."

Tess and Michowsky exchanged a quick glance. Myra Lambert had checked out of the hotel almost two hours later after Sanford had left Houston. Their strongest lead seemed to have a solid alibi. But was it real?

"If you need a more accurate answer, you can always check with the tower. I flew out of Intercontinental. They have the flight plan and all," he replied casually. "Now, if you'll excuse me, I'm already late for my next meeting."

He firmly shook their hands while maintaining good eye contact, then left them in the care of his assistant, a long-legged blonde in a gray business suit, the skirt only one inch longer than the jacket. She escorted them to the lobby without asking any questions, her professional smile seeming permanently etched on her lips.

"He fits the bill," Tess said, as soon as they climbed into Michowsky's SUV.

"Only he's got an ironclad alibi," Michowsky replied, visibly frustrated. "He was in the air at the time Myra checked out of her hotel."

Tess grinned. "Exactly," she replied. "He was in the air. But where?"

Michowsky glanced at her. "I'll be damned," he reacted. "What if he landed elsewhere and picked Myra up?"

"Or he could've said he left at ten and lied, but we have to speak with ATC at the Houston airport to verify that. Air traffic control has a log of all departures, arrivals, and flight plans. Miami should have a record of when he landed, what time that was."

"I didn't get the killer vibe from him," Michowsky said. "He's a cold-hearted bastard, *that* vibe was loud and clear, but do you see him as the man who could've raped and killed Myra?"

Tess paused for a long moment, going through the facts, validating the feeling in her gut.

"Did you notice the collection of plane photos on the wall?" Tess replied. "It's the same aircraft, over and over again, different settings, different times of day. It's always from the tarmac, never in flight, and not professionally taken. They seemed like phone photos to me."

"And? Maybe the man really loves his plane."

"I'm willing to bet these photos are the souvenirs he keeps after each murder."

"Nah . . . can't be. How many were there? Eighteen?"

"Yup," Tess replied. "Arranged as if he knows he will add more. And I'm afraid today's visit might've spooked him. We need to get a warrant for that plane really quickly. I promise you we'll find Myra's DNA all over that cabin."

"Who do you think will issue that warrant? No judge in

their right mind will risk antagonizing the Sanfords without a ton of evidence."

"That's why we have to start with the ATC. I'll ask the shift supervisor, if he were to kill someone like Myra was killed, how would he do it? Because I promise you, M, this is our unsub. I don't know how he pulled it off, how he picked her up without being seen, or how he got the cabin door to open mid-flight, but I know it in my gut, just like I know he killed many other women before Myra. Seventeen, to be exact."

"How come he was never connected to the missing persons cases before? Any analyst looking at victimology would've spotted Sanford as the point of convergence, common to all their backgrounds."

"We found a body, which changed things," Tess replied. "If Myra would've been a missing person, the investigation would've been handled differently. We would've mapped her last twenty-four hours, but being she was seen departing the hotel by herself *after* the Sanford meeting, we would've probably never looked at Sanford. We would've had no reason to look at other missing persons cases fitting Myra's profile. I'll ask Donovan to do a search and see how many open missing persons cases can be linked to Sanford, even if remotely."

They drove in silence for a long moment.

"I wonder if he knows we're on to him," Michowsky said.

"Oh, believe me, he knows," Tess replied. "And he'll make his move. We have to hurry."

12

MOVE

His smile froze and turned into a grimace of rage the moment the door closed behind the two cops.

How the hell had they found Myra? How? It wasn't supposed to happen, not in a million years. It had never happened before. He'd gone to extreme lengths to make sure of that. He'd dropped her almost two hundred miles from the shore, when the tides receded, so the currents would be carrying her farther away. She was bleeding and a fresh kill, shark bait ready to be preyed on. There wasn't a single vessel in sight, not for many miles. He knew, because he checked. He always checked.

None of the others were found, so why Myra? What were the odds of that?

He stood perfectly still, weighing his options.

They were close . . . if they'd got to him already, soon his entire system would unravel. How soon before they'd figure out some of his flights were significantly longer than others? How long before they interviewed his maintenance crew, to find out that sometimes he demanded full fuel tanks for relatively short flights?

And how long before they convinced a judge to issue a warrant to search his plane? They'd find everything they needed to lock him up forever. There had to be DNA from every girl he'd taken up there. For sure they'd find Myra's.

But what if he took off and never looked back?

He clenched his fists, ready to punch a hole in the wall to soothe his anger, but even that could be construed as evidence against him, so it was better to keep cool. Strangely enough, under the circumstances, the thing that infuriated him the most was the thought of Brittany, her long, sleek hair and the way it curled around her shoulders just like Geneva's, her inviting eyes, her bright smile. He could never take her now, just like he couldn't dream of taking Geneva anymore. No . . . if he ran away, that was it, end of story, and the bitch from hell would reign over his legacy undisturbed, sharing Sanford wealth with her bastard son. He'd be ostracized to some far land from where he could never return.

There would be other Brittanys where he was going, but no Geneva. The thought of leaving her behind to live and thrive unpunished burned him inside, his entire body revolting at the thought.

Choking down the bile in his throat, he decided even his wife wasn't worth the risk of spending the rest of his life in jail. With his difficult decision finally made, he opened the safe, hidden behind a massive painting on the wall, and started removing ten-thousand-dollar bundles, piling them on his desk. He'd stashed away a small fortune over the years, knowing the risks he was taking, knowing a day like this would eventually come.

He pressed a button on his phone, and his assistant's voice came to life within seconds. "Yes, Mr. Sanford?"

"Lindsey, could you bring me a large duffel bag?"

"Right away, sir."

While waiting for the duffel bag, one last thing remained: deciding where to go. A place that didn't extradite; that was a no-brainer. A warm place, because he loved the sun. A place where girls were sexy and feisty. A place where the local drug market would be willing to pay at least fifty cents on the dollar for his plane and thus ensure his carefree future.

He hated the thought of living in Africa, so that was off the list. Several European countries also refused to extradite, but life wasn't that great there, and neither was Russia or Ukraine. Venezuela popped into his mind; he could live like a king there, protected by his own army of mercenaries, but what kind of life would that be? That left few choices; a couple of Arab countries, like the United Arab Emirates or Saudi Arabia, but his sexual preferences would probably get him killed there in the shortest of time. The Maldives had excellent beaches, but he liked his women a certain way and the locals didn't fit the bill.

So, Venezuela it was going to be. His Gulfstream would make a fine addition to some drug lord's fleet, or maybe he'd start using it himself to haul product here and there. The girls were hot and willing, all fiery brunettes who always wanted to please men like him.

He called and ordered the jet fueled and ready in thirty minutes. From Miami, Venezuela was a quick flight over Cuba due south, only a couple of brief hours.

Lindsey delivered the requested duffel bag, standing in the doorway. To her obvious surprise, Richard sent her away before she could notice the pile of cash on his desk. He packed the duffel bag full of cash and still had to shove a couple of bundles in his pockets. From the top right drawer of his mahogany desk, he took his loaded handgun, an H&K P7, and tucked it inside his belt, after checking the ammo. Then he took his passport and gave his office one last look, his eyes lingering over the jet photo collection.

He had the digital photos on his phone. He could print them again.

And there would be other Brittanys.

And maybe, with the right connections, the Geneva problem could be eventually solved, even from a distance. He needed to learn to live vicariously through another where his wife was concerned. He'd make sure her death would be long, pained, and memorable.

He grabbed the heavy duffel bag and left the office in a hurried gait.

"I'll be in Houston for the afternoon," he told Lindsey, like he always did.

"Yes, sir," she acknowledged with a smile.

He took the elevator down and checked the lobby before proceeding. No sign of the cops, but his wife was there, defiant, a smirk on her lips the moment their eyes locked. Darkness engulfed his mind and sparked a fire in his groin.

He was being offered another chance. Fate was finally smiling on him.

Without thinking, he rushed to her and grabbed her arm. "Gen, I was just coming to get you," he said in a low voice. "It's your father. He collapsed in his Houston office."

Geneva's hand instantly covered her mouth, while tears sprung from her eyes. "Oh, no . . . Is he—?"

"Come on, I have the jet waiting for us," he said, rushing toward the entrance, where Lindsey already had his Porsche waiting.

He didn't dare look back to see if she followed him; she had to. It was his last chance, his only chance. She had to come.

Geneva opened the passenger door at the same time he got behind the wheel, probably too distraught to notice the glint of excitement in his eyes.

Soon, it would be just the two of them in the air, his dream come true.

Then Venezuela, and a brand-new life of freedom and pleasure.

13

TARMAC

"Let's go over what we know," Tess said, raising her voice the way she normally did when her words had to carry over the blaring sirens of Michowsky's SUV.

They'd been called to appear in front of the judge, the old prune refusing to sign the warrant presented by Donovan. Afraid to upset the third richest man in the state of Florida, His Honor had requested their appearance to argue the facts in support of the warrant request.

"ATC confirmed that Sanford took off three days ago from Houston Intercontinental, but Houston Executive Airport has him landing shortly thereafter, only to take off again at twelve thirty P.M. Which means he could've made the stop to hide his tracks and create the perfect alibi."

"Sleight of hand," Tess replied. "He gives everyone the big airport alibi, while he picks up his victims at Houston Executive, unknown and unseen."

"Exactly. We know now, the cab company confirmed, that Myra was dropped at Houston Executive, not Intercontinental. The cabbie's log said, 'Airport,' but the cab company pulled the GPS logs."

"Donovan is running backgrounds on all missing persons reports in both Houston and Miami," Tess said, sounding a little tense. "No results yet."

Michowsky's phone rang, and he took the call with a press on a steering wheel button.

"He's on the move," the caller announced.

Michowsky had placed two plainclothes cops at Sanford Wilkes to keep tabs on Richard Sanford.

"Alone?" Tess asked.

"No, with the missus," the cop said.

"Stay on him like fleas on a pound dog," Michowsky said.

"Copy that," the man said, then the call ended.

"I've got a bad feeling about this," Tess said.

Sanford wasn't the kind of man to keep his scheduled meetings while waiting on the cops to catch up with him. He wasn't going to go down without a fight, without trying to run. He must've had an escape plan all along, and it probably involved the damn company jet.

She knew hers would, if she were in his place.

The one question she couldn't answer was, why flee with his wife? That was the wrench in her understanding of his logic, the one fact that potentially changed everything. The two socialites weren't particularly famous for their closely knit marriage; quite the opposite, as Tess was learning from a quick internet search on her phone. There had been instances in which Geneva Wilkes had famously insulted her husband in public, the insult exacerbated dramatically and publicized in the tabloids.

Also known as a trigger, the event that fueled a psychopath's unraveling, his desire to kill, was usually victims who resembled the object of the psychopath's rage.

She pulled up a photo of Geneva Wilkes on her phone, then whistled.

"What?" Michowsky asked.

"His wife," Tess replied, "is an older version of Myra. Same hair, eyes, oval face." She pressed her lips together, thinking. She had to give Donovan the physiognomy characteristics; it was a safe bet this new information would help with narrowing the unsub's victim list. "Turn around," she said.

"Now?" Michowsky reacted.

"Yes, now," she replied. "Once he gets on that plane, we won't see him again. If we look really hard, we'll find Geneva Wilkes floating or sinking somewhere in the Gulf, in about two hours when he's finished with her. She's been his trigger all along, fueling his rage."

Michowsky slammed on the brakes and pulled a wheel-screeching 180, then floored it, heading to Miami International.

Michowsky's phone rang again, just as Tess was about to dial the Miami International ATC.

"We're at the airport, but we can't pursue anymore, not without prejudice," the cop announced. "They had private card access to the VIP tarmac, where their plane is already waiting, engines running. Unless I break down the gate and shut down the entire airport—"

"Get that gate open," Michowsky shouted. "Now, damn it!"

"Ten-four," the cop replied and ended the call.

"Unbelievable," Michowsky swore under his breath.

Tess dialed the Miami International ATC and requested to speak with the shift supervisor, the same man she'd spoken with only an hour earlier, the one who had confirmed the landing times for the most recent Sanford jet flights.

"Mr. McRay, Agent Winnett here with the FBI," she announced. "You have the Sanford corporate jet on the tarmac, correct?"

"Yes, it just filed a flight plan for Houston, requesting immediate departure. He's cleared."

"You'll have to revoke that clearance and ground the plane," she said. "It's a matter of life and death."

A short moment of silence, then McRay replied, "I'm afraid I can't do that without due process, Agent Winnett. We can't just ground planes like that. Not anymore. The times have changed."

"But you can delay their departure, can't you?"

"Um, I guess I could do that, yes, ma'am."

When they pulled up at the VIP gate, the two cops were talking with three airport security personnel. By their body language and the closed tarmac gate, it wasn't going too well. Beyond that gate and almost entirely hidden behind the terminal, the Sanford jet was slowly rolling.

"Damn son of a bitch," she muttered, and started dialing the ATC, but McRay's call came in first.

"They're not cleared, but they're rolling anyway," he announced. "There's nothing I can do at this point, Agent Winnett. It's in your hands now."

She ended the call with an angry tap on the red button, then said, "Bust though the damn gate, M. Let's catch the bastard."

Michowsky pulled back then floored it, ignoring the shouting coming from airport security. "Hold on," he warned, a second before the impact. "Airbags will deploy."

She held on tightly, forcing her head against the headrest as Michowsky plowed through the reinforced gate. The SUV swerved and jumped off its wheels as the airbags deployed, blinding them for a moment. Powder from the airbags filled the cabin, suffocating her and stinging her eyes.

Tess rolled down her window and batted the deflating airbags until she had an unobstructed view of the tarmac through the cracked windshield.

"The damn thing is gaining speed," Tess shouted.

Michowsky held the wheel with white-knuckled hands,

heading straight for the jet on the empty taxiway. They started gaining on it, not by much, but enough to put the jet within firing range.

Tess pulled out her Sig and cocked it, then took aim at the departing jet, leaning through the open window.

"What are you doing?" Michowsky reacted. "You'll blow the damn thing to smithereens."

"Aiming for the wheels, M. Just go steady and take me as close as you can."

Her voice was calm as she replied, but she felt the sweat lining her palms. Missing her intended target by just a little bit could make the bullet hit the fuel tanks or one of the engines, and the jet could explode, killing Richard Sanford and Geneva Wilkes.

She breathed in, exhaled half the air in her lungs, then held her breath, and fired. The first bullet hit one of the right wheels, instantly deflating it, sending pieces of torn tire at them. The jet continued though, the second wheel still holding the plane level.

"I can't go any faster," Michowsky announced.

The jet was still on the taxiway, but it was accelerating as if getting ready for takeoff. It was probably Sanford's intention to take off from the taxiway, not planning to make his way to the runway anymore.

She looked at Michowsky's speedometer and groaned. They were already going 145 miles per hour, which meant the Gulfstream could essentially lift off at any time.

She breathed in again, steadying herself, and remembered the words of her firing range instructor. "Slow is fast," the man had taught her. And since then, she hadn't missed too many shots.

She aimed for the second wheel on the right gear assembly. She exhaled halfway, held her breath, and fired. This time, the pierced tire exploded, and the jet veered suddenly, crossing over into the next taxiway and coming to a stop with roaring reversed engines.

"Whoa," Michowsky said, barely avoiding the wing of the turning plane.

They pulled near the Gulfstream's closed door and took positions close to it, weapons drawn. The other two cops caught up with them and took their positions behind the open doors of their unmarked vehicle.

For a few long moments, nothing happened.

"You can't stay on that plane forever, Sanford," Winnett shouted.

Another long moment of silence, while the jet's engines were idling. The smell of burned rubber and jet fuel filled the hot, midday air.

Then the plane's door opened, the steps hitting the asphalt. She didn't see Sanford at first; then he appeared, holding his wife by the throat in an armlock and pressing a gun to her head. She was choking, grasping at his arm with feeble, flailing hands.

"I'll kill her, you know I will," Sanford shouted.

"And you'll fry for it," Tess announced calmly. "You're not going anywhere but jail, and you know it. This is the end of the line, Sanford. You're permanently grounded."

"I'll fry anyway, won't I?"

"You don't have to," Tess replied. "Look, I'll trade you," she offered, holding her weapon in the air, then slowly holstering it. "Her life for mine, and the promise you won't fry."

She kept her hands in the air, waiting for his decision.

"Winnett, what the hell?" Michowsky said under his breath. "Don't do this. We have SWAT on the way. They'll put a bullet through his head, and we all get to go home for dinner tonight."

"I know what I'm doing, M," she whispered, not taking her eyes off of Sanford. "I need to know."

"What?"

"Who the others were, and how many."

"All right," Sanford replied, shoving Geneva down the aircraft steps and training his gun on Tess. "Get up here."

Geneva tumbled and fell, screaming as she hit the ground. Sanford grinned, a flicker of mad excitement in his eyes seeing her hurt.

One of the cops helped Geneva get up and limp out of the way. When she was safely away, Tess slowly approached the plane, careful to put herself between Michowsky's weapon and Sanford's body. She couldn't allow him to die before answering a few questions.

Once she reached the top of the stairs, he grabbed her arm and forced her inside. His eyes were dark, the tension in his face turning his muscles into knots that danced under his skin.

"How many were there, Sanford?"

"I don't know what you're talking about," he replied calmly, his body language showing no signs of deception.

Psychopaths rarely showed the same adrenaline-fueled signs of deception that other people did, because they don't feel guilt, remorse, or the fear of being caught. To them, truth or lie is the same, a series of words they speak with the purpose of reaching a certain goal.

"I believe eighteen, but I'm not sure if you had the time to hang the photo taken after Myra's flight," Tess added.

"Why would I tell you anything?" he asked, shoving the

barrel of his gun in the side of her throat. She choked and coughed, then replied, "So you don't fry. That's your only chance. Full cooperation with me, and we won't treat you as a maximum risk detainee."

"I'd still be locked up, wouldn't I?" he said. "No deal."

She groaned and forced herself to smile, looking in his blood-lusting eyes. "I thought you were smarter than that, Mr. Sanford."

"Talk," he commanded coldly.

"People like you, I mean, people with means like yours, could arrange for a prisoner breakout during transport to or from the courthouse. Then another private plane can remove you out of the country within hours. We'd never catch up with you. But for that, you'd want to be classified a certain way. If we classify you as capital offender, you get max security and that jail break won't happen."

She could see the wheels turning in his mind. The gun's pressure against her neck had decreased, and he shifted his weight from one foot to the other, invigorated.

Hope, no matter how unrealistic and crazy, was a powerful weapon.

"Oh, and you'd need a trustworthy helper, someone who wouldn't hesitate to break the law for you," she added, pausing for a beat. "Someone like the man who cleans up for you. The one who took care of Myra's cabbie," she ventured, shooting in the dark and from the hip.

Myra's cabbie having a stroke seemed a little too convenient for her taste, and she was willing to bet there was more to it than just the man's age and drinking habits. The timing of that stroke had been too perfect.

Sanford didn't flinch and didn't push back in any way.

"Do you think he'll break you out of jail if you pay him well?" she pushed.

He nodded. "What do you want in return?"

"The names of all the girls you killed," Tess replied coldly. "That's to make me look good to my boss," she added, afraid he might back out of the deal if she seemed too zealous. "And some cash for me, enough to secure my future. Say, ten million?"

He nodded again. "Five now, five when I break out of jail," he said.

"Deal," Tess replied. "Write down those names, then let's get out of here."

He unzipped the duffel bag, leaving his gun on a table across the aisle. He pulled out a notepad and a pen and started writing names. He wrote and wrote, the list much longer than eighteen or nineteen.

"How many?" Tess asked, almost whispering, her voice strangled in horror. His calm demeanor made it worse; his complete lack of emotion when it came to the lives he took was too hard to stomach, even for her, even if she knew the reason for it.

"Twenty-seven," he replied, pushing the piece of paper her way. "Since this one," he added, underlining one of the names, "I had someone help me clean up. Witnesses and such. So, there are more names, but you only wanted the girls. My girls."

He closed the duffel bag zipper and pushed it toward her with his foot. "It's your business how you get this out of here unseen. It's five-point-three million. The moment I'm free, my guy will make sure you get the rest."

She nodded, feeling she couldn't breathe in the warm air ripe with jet exhaust. But she knew that was in her mind, the thing keeping her from filling her lungs being the immense revulsion she felt for the killer staring at her.

"I'll need your gun," she said, extending her hand, "and I'll need you to surrender to me now, so we avoid you getting shot by overzealous SWAT members."

He stared at her for a brief moment, but she held his glance without hesitation. She wasn't a psychopath, but in this case, she felt no remorse and no fear for what she was about to do.

Apparently convinced, he handed over his gun, which she tucked in her belt. He allowed her to cuff him, without resisting.

Then Tess walked to the open plane door and shouted, "Hold your fire, we're coming out."

She walked him down the stairs, then turned him over to Michowsky.

"There's a case with five mil inside the plane; log that into evidence. It will cover the gate and your Interceptor."

Sanford stared at Tess with widened eyes.

She continued, while a smile curled her lip. "Book him as a capital offender, maximum security."

"Hey, you promised I won't fry," he shouted, while Michowsky hauled him to the SUV.

She opened the back door, making room for Michowsky to load him. Then she leaned in at his ear and whispered, "I lied."

Michowsky closed the door and wiped his hands on his pants, as if to remove any traces left on his skin by the contact with Sanford. Then he turned to her, grinning widely.

"We don't fry people in Florida anymore; we gas them. I'm sure you know that."

She waved away his feigned concern.

"Don't worry, he'll find out soon enough."

Did *Mile High Death* keep you riveted to the pages as you raced through the story, gasping at every twist? Find out what happens next for Tess Winnett and her team, in the next unmissable Leslie Wolfe thriller.

Read on for previews from:

The Girl They Took

A completely gripping, heart-stopping crime thriller.

*** and ***

A Beautiful Couple

He's a charismatic TV anchor with everything to lose. She's the perfect wife, desperate to protect their life. But after one fatal mistake, their picture-perfect world starts to unravel.

Thank You!

A big, heartfelt thank you for choosing to read my book. If you enjoyed it, please take a moment to leave me a four or five-star review; I would be very grateful. It doesn't need to be more than a couple of words, and it makes a huge difference.

Join my mailing list to receive special offers, exclusive bonus content, and news about upcoming new releases. Use the button below, visit www.LeslieWolfe.com to sign up, or email me at LW@WolfeNovels.com.

Did you enjoy *Mile High Death*? Would you like to see some of these characters return? Which ones? Your thoughts and feedback are very valuable to me. Please contact me directly through one of the channels listed below. Email works best: LW@WolfeNovels.com or use the button below:

If you haven't already, check out *Dawn Girl*, a gripping, heart stopping crime thriller and the first book in the Tess Winnett series. If you enjoyed *Criminal Minds*, you'll enjoy *Dawn Girl*. Or, if you're in a mood for something lighter, try *Las Vegas Girl*; you'll love it.

Connect With Me

Amazon.com/LeslieWolfe

LW@WolfeNovels.com

Amazon.com/stores/Leslie-Wolfe/author/B00KR1QZ0G

LeslieWolfe.com

Facebook.com/wolfenovels

Instagram.com/Wolfe.Leslie

TikTok.com/@Leslie.Wolfe

Bookbub.com/authors.leslie-wolfe

Preview: *The Girl They Took*

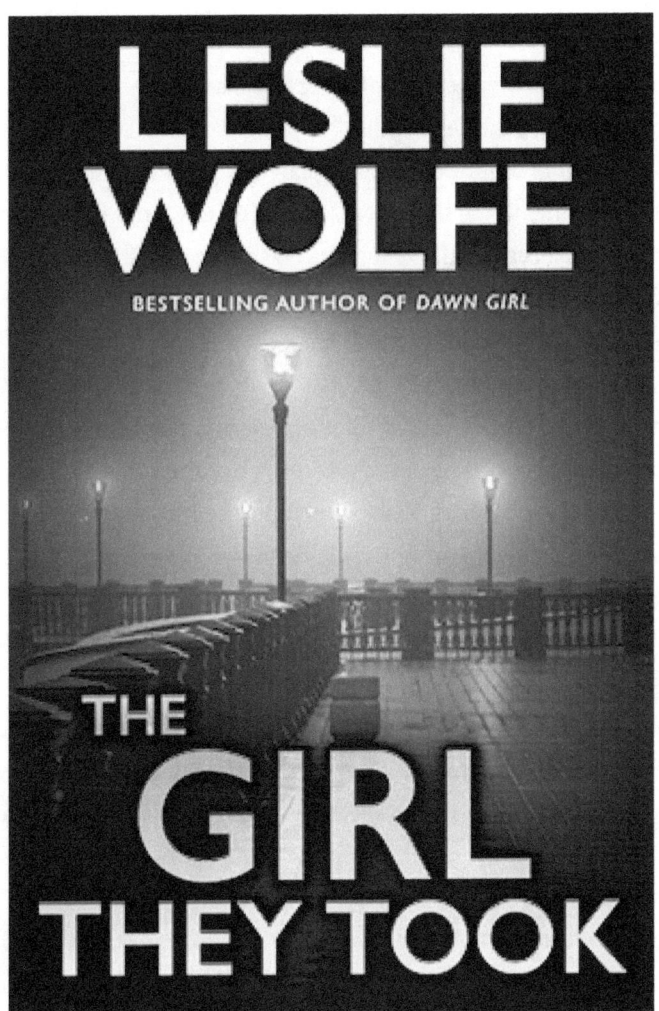

1

GONE

Seven minutes before curtain raise, her daughter Paige had the worst case of the hiccups.

The small cast of the school play was gathered around her, and that only made things worse. Her Paige wasn't one to love an audience, especially when she wasn't up to par for the task. She'd hid her glittery face against Miriam's jeans and refused to leave the comfort of her mother's leg.

"I'm so sorry," Miriam had said, looking at the teacher, Mrs. Langhorne. The woman smiled, feigning understanding and compassion, when her eyes glinted with impatient irritation as if it were Miriam's fault Paige had the hiccups. Or Paige's even. "I tried everything. I gave her water, the other teacher, Mr.—"

"Mowrey, yes," Mrs. Langhorne replied, shooting her wristwatch another concerned look.

"Yes, he tried to talk her out of it." Mrs. Langhorne sighed, tapping her heel impatiently against the scratched, wooden floor of the theater backstage. "This is not exactly a Broadway show if you know what I mean," Miriam pleaded in a lower voice. "We can be a few minutes late if need be."

The woman rolled her eyes, a quick gesture she tried to hide under her long lashes and a quick turn of her head to the side. "This is the Universal Stage Theater." She sounded as if she was about to choke on her own indignation. "The school went through a lot of trouble to secure this venue on a Saturday evening, Mrs. Welsh. We might as well behave accordingly and be on time."

Miriam pressed her lips tightly together, gently caressing her daughter's curly, red hair and counting the seconds between hiccups. She wished she could tell that woman everything that was crossing her mind at the time but couldn't. Not if she wanted Paige to continue to attend the classes of the exclusive St. Moritz school. Even at the ridiculous tuition they were charging, the waiting lists were a mile long, and kids had their names on them since birth. That was, of course, if parents could make the commitment to pay fifty grand a year for their offspring's exclusive education.

Two other children, including the little boy who played Hansel, whispered something and giggled, shooting her daughter amused looks. Paige whimpered against her leg, the barely noticeable sound interrupted by a loud "Hic."

"Let me try something, if I may," a man asked in a low whisper, approaching from a dressing room. He was dressed for the stage and wore a mask and woodworker's coveralls with fake stains applied with stage makeup. Through the holes of the mask, his eyes seemed like anthracite.

Miriam looked at her watch and groaned. Two minutes until curtain raise. "Sure."

The man took Paige's hand gently and waited until the little girl look at him. "Wanna get rid of these hiccups so we can do the play and go home and watch TV?" He still whispered, no one else but the three of them privy to their conversation.

Paige nodded. "Hic."

The man held his hands in the air and looked at Miriam briefly as if asking permission again. "Hiccups are nothing but spasms of the diaphragm. Sometimes," he touched Paige's stomach right under her sternum with one expertly placed finger, "all you have to do is push the right button." He held his finger pressed against Paige's diaphragm for a few seconds, then took a step back. "Done." He grabbed both Paige's hands into his. "I'm willing to bet you one dollar you won't be hiccupping again today." There was laughter in his whispered voice.

Paige seemed disappointed. Maybe it was the thought of the dollar she wasn't going to earn, or perhaps she had stage fright like Miriam suspected.

Crouching by her side, Miriam arranged her long, auburn curls and straightened her costume. She'd inherited Miriam's hair and complexion. She quickly wiped a fleck of glitter off her nose and put a swift kiss on her freckled cheek.

"Mom," Paige protested, shooting the other kids an embarrassed look.

So soon. She was only eight.

Mrs. Langhorne clapped her hands in typical foreman-on-the-floor style, steering the kids toward their places for curtain raise.

Rushing to her seat and trying to step on the balls of her feet to keep the clicking of her high heels to a minimum, Miriam barely got there in time for curtain raise. She had an aisle seat, and the one next to her was still empty. Max, her husband, wasn't there yet. She checked her phone and saw a text message apologizing for a work-related delay that couldn't be avoided.

Across from the aisle, another empty seat caught her attention. Paige's father, Darrel, hadn't arrived either. Miriam swallowed a bitter sigh. Tonight, Paige would learn how to act in front of a sizeable audience and how to deal with disappointment.

The theater was large, equipped with comfortable plush

seats spaced to leave plenty of legroom. Miriam sunk in her seat, happy to be off her feet after what had seemed an endless day. She'd worked a few hours that morning, dealing with a staffing shortage at the pharmacy, then had rushed home to fix lunch and get Paige ready for the performance. They'd rehearsed lines together the entire week, to the point where Miriam had dreamt she was Gretel herself one night. She was beyond ready to be done with the school play, but it had been a wonderful opportunity for her to spend more time with her daughter. Thankfully, all she had to do after lunch and a quick nap for Paige was her hair, her nails with plenty of glitter, and another fitting of her costume, with last-minute sewing of hidden clasps required to keep the darn thing in place.

But Paige looked beautiful as Gretel, her long hair brought forward on her shoulders, her freckles picture-perfect, her starched white apron shining over her burgundy gathered skirt with ruffles, her smile beaming, full of confidence. Of course, that was at home, in the sanctity of her own bedroom. As soon as they'd reached the majestic theater, everything changed. She started trembling at first, then she needed the restroom three times in twenty-five minutes. Then the hiccups came.

But it was all sorted out now, and Miriam could rest for a few minutes. Thankfully, Paige's appearance on the stage was flawless, her first lines perfectly articulated, her voice strong, fearless. Whatever stage fright monsters had plagued her were gone as if they'd never existed.

Her little girl was a natural.

Mouthing the lines as Paige acted them, Miriam held back tears. Something tugged at her heart seeing her little girl there, vulnerable and brave in front of all those people, elbows locked with the boy who played Hansel, playfully jumping and walking in circles on her thin legs as if the whole world was hers. She was growing up so fast... too fast. Soon she'd be gone, a young woman with a life of her own, a house of her own, children of her own.

Among enthusiastic cheering from the gathering of parents, a gentle tap on her shoulder got her attention. "Excuse me, ma'am?"

She turned. A man leaned toward her to keep his voice down and still be heard while speaking with her. "Yes?"

"Do you have a red Subaru, with the tag number, um," he read from a note in his hand, "GHR-G12?"

She frowned. She'd never been able to remember her tag, but she'd driven her burgundy Subaru Forester tonight. "Yes, what's wrong?"

The man straightened his back, but not completely, still hunched forward, his hands clasped together. "I'm so sorry, ma'am, but I'm afraid I caused it some damage when I pulled out of the lot." He threw a look over his shoulder. "The usher told me where to find you."

She sighed, screwing her eyes shut for a brief moment. One minute of peace, and it had to be shattered by this klutz who couldn't drive straight for the life of him. Son of a bitch. At least he'd had the sense to own up to his crap, instead of disappearing and leaving her with a dent or whatever, to fix on her own. That much deserved some respect.

She threw Paige a regretful look, wishing she didn't have to leave the play to deal with the car nonsense. At least Paige wasn't paying attention to her, engulfed in her act, spreading confetti as breadcrumbs from her cute little brown satchel.

Miriam stood and followed the man who kept walking with his shoulders hunched forward and his head lowered as if begging forgiveness with every fiber of his body. It was rare to see someone acting like that these days when people didn't have decent morals anymore.

She turned toward the theater exit, but the man gently touched her elbow. "Follow me; it's shorter this way," he said, pointing toward a half-lit corridor that led to the now-closed coffee shop. Frowning, she tried to remember where she'd parked. By the time they arrived, the front parking lot was full, and she'd parked on the side, but which side? Torn between wanting to get back into her seat and some unnerving gut feeling, she hesitated but eventually gave in. The man, wearing a dark jacket zipped up to his chin, seemed kind, humble even, deeply embarrassed to find himself in that situation. He wore a ball cap that shaded his eyes in the dim light, but Miriam could tell he was smiling apologetically, showing two rows of teeth slightly stained by tobacco use. His beard was trim and dark, not a strand of gray in it. He must've been young, maybe even younger than her.

As they approached the door, her footsteps resounding loudly on the marble corridor, he fell behind a little as if getting ready to hold the door for her and let her exit first. "After you, ma'am," he'd said in a strangely excited voice.

That was the last thing she remembered before everything went dark. The half-baked question about that nuance in his voice. Why the excitement? What was he—

Then the blow to her head that had sent shards of light in her skull before darkness took ahold of her mind.

When she came to, she was lying on the floor in what must've been the theater's janitorial closet, the smell of Pine-Sol and chlorine bleach unmistakable. Pitch dark except for a faint sliver of light coming in under the door, it was enough for

Miriam to get grounded. Ignoring the thumping in her skull, she rose to her feet and tried the door handle, silently praying.

It opened without any resistance.

A thought zapped like lightning through her mind, leaving her breathless, her heart beating hard and fast against her rib cage.

Paige.

She ran all the way back through the corridor, noticing things were slightly different. Most lights were off now. There was an eerie silence, where before, there used to be music coming from the stage, the high-pitched voices of the children, and the rhythmic clapping of the audience. Now the only rhythm she could hear was the frenetic beating of her own heart and the clacking of her high-heeled boots against the marble as she was rushing to find her little girl.

When she finally reached the auditorium entrance, she gasped. The doors were wide open, and the auditorium was shrouded in darkness.

Where her daughter had played Gretel in front of a cheering audience, only two faint stage lights remained. The theater was deserted and eerily silent; the only sound she could hear was her own heart, pounding in a frenzy against her chest.

"Paige," she called loudly, and the echo of her voice reverberated in the wide, empty space.

For a moment, she considered searching the backstage area where she'd last been with Paige before the play had started, but it made no sense. Those rooms were a mere curtain away, and not a sound came from there.

She rushed toward the main entrance and pushed the massive glass door. It opened after opposing a brief resistance, and an alarm sounded. She stepped outside and stopped sharply at the top of the stairs, stunned, her blood turned to icicles. Darkness had fallen, thick and filled with ocean mist, lampposts like ghosts sprinkling yellow haloes against the sky.

The place where she'd parked her car was deserted, as was the entire parking lot. She was the only one there.

Paige was gone. They'd taken her little girl.

Like *The Girl They Took*?

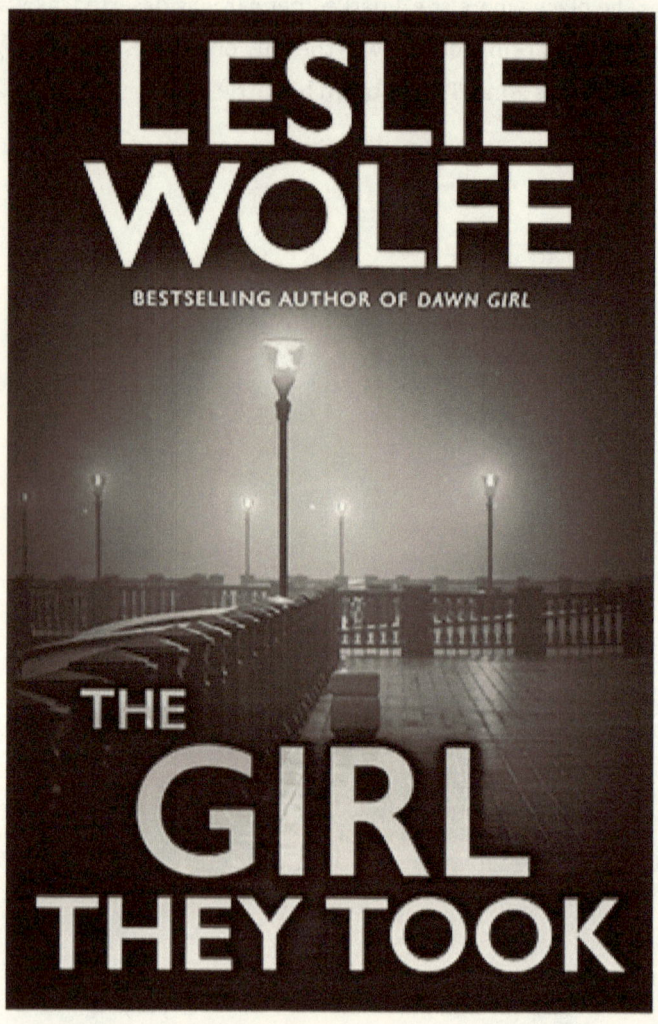

LESLIE WOLFE

BESTSELLING AUTHOR OF *DAWN GIRL*

THE GIRL THEY TOOK

Buy it now!

Preview: *A Beautiful Couple*

1

AMANDA DAVIS

I killed a man.

The surreal words fill my mind, echoing in shock and fear with tremors that weaken my body. As reality starts setting in, I gasp silently, covering my mouth with a trembling hand, stifling a sob. Wide-eyed, I stare at the body lying in a motionless heap at the bottom of the stairs, disbelief clinging to me in scattered thoughts and anxious breaths.

It can't be true. He can't be dead.

But I can see it's all too real. In his neck, twisted and crooked sideways in an impossible posture. In the sickening crack of broken bones I remember hearing just as he was landing on the hardwood floor after bouncing down the steep flight of stairs. In the pooling blood that's slowly seeping from his head, gleaming burgundy under the yellowish light coming from the floor lamp by the door.

A noise outside makes me jump out of my skin. Someone's coming. I freeze in place at the top of the stairs, my fingers white-knuckled on the handrail, as the footsteps draw closer. Then, in the dark frame of the living room window, the profile of a woman appears, her face dimly lit as she passes by. Without turning her head to look inside.

I breathe.

Then I realize someone could've seen what happened. A passerby. A neighbor. Anyone.

I force some air into my lungs to steel my fraught nerves. Still holding on to the handrail for support, I climb down the stairs, careful not to slip, as if his fall could repeat somehow and seal my fate in vengeful symmetry, my body next to his. I hold my breath as I approach, senselessly hoping he's still alive, yet fearing it. When I eventually breathe, the metallic smell of blood fills my nostrils, filling me with dread.

I rush to the window and close the blinds, then peek outside between two slats. The street is eerily deserted and still. For now.

Crouching by his side, I feel for a pulse with frozen fingers. Touching his skin sears me, prickling the back of my head as if he could snap out of death and grab my shaky wrist.

There's no pulse.

His golf shirt is soaked with blood at the collar and smells faintly of aftershave, although his face shows a two-day stubble. His skull is fractured where it must've hit the edge of a step, the indentation clearly visible through his buzz-cut hair despite the bleeding laceration. Reluctantly, I slip my fingers and trace his neck, wincing as I find the protruding vertebra, a sign of a fractured cervical spine resulting in a fatal spinal cord injury.

He died the moment he hit the floor.

I'm more than qualified to make that statement. It doesn't change how I feel, though. Unsure of myself. Scared. Unsteady. My heart is racing, and my chest is tightening, as if the walls of this room are drawing closer and closer, about to squeeze the life out of me.

The sound of an approaching car makes me rush to the window and peek outside. It doesn't slow down until it reaches the corner and turns, tinting the darkness with hues of bright taillight red.

I turn on my heels and stare at the body, unsure what to do.

His eyes are still open, as if looking straight through me with hypnotizing, dilated pupils. It chills the blood in my veins. Barely touching him with the tips of my fingers, I crouch down and close his eyelids swiftly, shaking, eager to put some distance between me and him. I stand quickly and step back, feeling for the handrail, unable to take my eyes off of him. Part of me still expects him to get up and grab me, slam me against the wall, then put his hands around my throat and squeeze until my world goes dark. Just as his is now.

But he doesn't move. He's dead.

I killed him.

The enormity of what I've done weighs heavily on my heart. How could I let this happen?

It seems I had no choice, and yet, the truth is I *had* a choice, and I made the wrong one. That didn't happen a few moments ago, when I pushed him down the stairs.

No.

It happened earlier. Much earlier.

And now, I have to deal with the consequences of what I've done.

My first thought is to run, to put as much distance as I possibly can between me and the body lying on the blood-soaked floor. But there's no running away from this. Not right now. Not without a plan.

Still walking backward, my heel stops against the bottom step of the staircase and I nearly trip. I let myself slide down and sit on a step. For a moment of respite, my elbows rest on my shaky knees and my face lands in my hands, hiding from the grim sight.

Perhaps I could stall things for a few days before they come for me, because I know they will. Clinging to that glimmer of hope, my mind starts working. I raise my weary head and look around, taking inventory of everything I could use to buy myself some time. There isn't much.

One thing's certain: I have to get rid of the body.

That's when I realize I need help.

He's massive, at least six-three and well-built, weighing perhaps two-forty or about that much. It's what I liked about him... the strength, the agility, the apparent stamina and self-confidence. However, I'm not nearly that tall, and I'm one-forty at the most, on a bad, bloated day. I reach for his leg to test my strength, but stop before touching his ankle. It's pointless to even try. At work, it takes six of us to transfer a patient his size from the stretcher onto the bed.

I take out my phone and turn it on. The bitten apple lights up white on the black screen, then vanishes, making room for a picture of my son. Tristan just turned nine; we took that pic last summer, on the Santa Monica Pier. Seeing his piercing blue eyes touched by his enchanted smile brings the threat of tears to my eyes.

What if I lose him? What if they lock me up and I never see him again?

I can't bear the thought of that; it guts me. *No... I can't lose my son. It won't happen. Whatever it takes.*

I push the grim thoughts away and breathe deeply while putting in the passcode. His face disappears off the screen.

It will be all right. But the words I tell myself fail to reassure me.

As the screen fills with apps, I realize there's only one person I can call for the kind of help I need. The one person I'd rather never call or see again. My fingers falter retrieving the name from the contacts list. Hesitating, I give the fallen body another look, desperately wondering if there's any other way.

There isn't.

I brace myself for the questions that are about to come my way like machine gun bullets, merciless and cold and ripping through me in rapid-fire sequence.

Then I make the call, knowing that as soon as I share what I've done, there will be no turning back. My entire existence will be at the mercy of someone else. Someone I know I can't trust.

As the line rings in my ear, I reflect bitterly on the last few weeks, on everything that's happened.

I never wanted any of this.

All I wanted was a stupid divorce.

2

PAUL DAVIS

Two weeks ago

Hot damn. Tits like those should be illegal.

I touch my tie knot briefly, wishing I could loosen it a little. Instead, I end up straightening it—a reflex when I know I'm directly in camera view. Only, there's no camera trained on me. Not yet.

The cameras are all huddled outside the ballroom, where the guests keep arriving in their fancy cars and rental limos to attend the annual *Citizens Against Impaired Driving* fundraiser I'm chairing. Even so, I should be focusing on the people seated at the table with me, including my wife Amanda. But no...I can't focus on any of them.

Only on her, the stranger who captured my interest the moment we arrived at the venue. She's walking across the atrium with a sway of her hips, so rhythmic and smooth that it's as if she's dancing her way through to the light music in the background. Her satin gown hugs her perfect shape, taut over her perky, little breasts. A high leg slit lets me put eyes on more of her skin than my wife would appreciate. Good thing Amanda's not looking at me right now. She's chatting with an older woman seated next to her while I get to feast my eyes on the unsuspecting stranger.

The woman doesn't look my way, and I'm not used to being ignored. To feeling invisible. I hate how it makes me feel. I almost want to shout, "Hey, I'm here," but there's no point. I'd make an ass of myself. As she makes her way to the open bar, she turns away, and I can see that gown is a backless wonder, seemingly clinging only to her shoulders...and so lightly, I could make it fall off of her with the touch of a finger. The thought unsettles me. I shift in my seat. And keep watching.

Her back is just as perfect as everything else she's strutting. The dress, a deep shade of red, shimmers under the dim lights, generously draped and still tight over her ass. It dips daringly below the small of her flawless back. I can't keep my eyes off her.

I bet she's not wearing anything underneath that thing. For a moment, I imagine how it would feel to touch her smooth, glowing skin. How that perfectly shaped back would arch when I took her from behind. How she'd look at me after, laying spent on crumpled sheets, with her wavy, chestnut hair spread on my pillow.

She disappears from sight as a couple of men trail after her and block my view. They're probably sucked in by her wake, empty drink glasses in hand and following her like panting dogs on the prowl. I'm about to down my drink and give myself a reason to visit the open bar where she's headed, but my glass freezes in mid-air when I notice Amanda's eyes, drilling into me with barely contained rage.

She leans toward me until her breath touches my skin. "Really, Paul?" she whispers in my ear, faking a smile for whoever might be looking at us just now. "With me here? With all these people watching?"

My teeth grit as I set my glass down. I hate being scolded like I'm four. "I didn't do anything," I growl back in a low voice, hating myself for saying it, for making excuses. She doesn't reply. Just sits there smiling, pretending everything is okay, but her chest is heaving, and her lower lip is trembling slightly.

But I'm still angry.

I'll admit I can get pissed off easily.

I take a sip of bourbon to hide the emotion, and pretend to pay some attention to what an overly bejeweled, middle-aged woman across the ten-person table is telling me. But it's pointless; I'm too frustrated to care. She goes on and on about a nephew of hers who died, and I'm forced to sit here, nod, and take it. She makes sweet eyes at me, and I fear I'll be throwing up in my mouth soon. I wash away the bad taste with more bourbon, then continue to smile and nod every now and then as she tells her endless story. Soon enough, she'll write me a check.

That's why I'm here, for the *Citizens Against Impaired Driving* annual fundraiser, gracefully hosted in the university atrium. The vast room is lavishly decorated with cascading white flowers set on every ten-person table, placed at the center of fine, white table linen. We're seated on dressed-up chairs tied up with satin ribbons. The myriad lights are dimly shining above us from chandelier-like, modern LED fixtures featuring intricate layers of crystal-clear prisms that glimmer in flickers of rainbow. These are not the drab, fluorescent university atrium lights I remember from my prior visits. They must've had them replaced for tonight. They really went over the top this time. I'm impressed.

The sound of my wife's laughter catches my attention. She looks beautiful tonight, with her long, blond hair done perfectly so, and she captures the undivided attention of at least two men. And I'm supposed to be okay with that. As if she can read my mind, her hand lands on my forearm. I pull away, instinctively, the thought of being seen as my wife's attachment bothering me on a deep level.

The air hums with low-key chatter and the occasional drunken burst of laughter. Because, of course, what's more fitting for a sobriety organization event than an open bar?

The event is sponsored generously and advertised for free by Golden State Broadcasting, the TV station I work for. They make sure that all invitation-only attendees can afford to fork out at least a couple grand for the four-course gourmet meal and said open bar. And the privilege to mingle with television people and the few Hollywood stars in attendance, and perhaps get a selfie with someone famous.

And as the president of *Citizens Against Impaired Driving* for the past few years, I'm at the center of all of it, soon to take the stage for the final speech of the evening, as soon as the guests finish their desserts.

Yet, I'm annoyed as fuck.

My boss, Raymond Cook, the president and CEO of Golden State Broadcasting, is a balding bundle of blundering ego. This year, the fourth in the pained history of his favorite event, he decided that the most prominent people in the station be seated with random donors, to engage them in conversation and have them imbibing and star-struck by the time they sign those checks. For what it's worth, he was fair; he's seated with donors, too. But he doesn't have unfuckable women drooling all over him while his wife is seated by his side. And that's not because he's not married. It's because no one really knows who Raymond Cook is. And no one cares.

But Paul Davis? That's a different story.

3

PAUL DAVIS

I'm the face of the evening news and the brains behind it. I'm the lead anchor, and there's a reason for that. On the evenings I'm working, the Nielsen ratings go up, ad revenue climbs by at least ten percent, and viewership and engagement both spike. Yes, I'll admit that the spike is mostly reflecting women, and I'm secretly pleased with it.

With ratings like that, I got my own show two years ago. It's a fifteen-minute interview attached to the end of the news program, called *The Final Question*. There's no co-anchor involved; just me and whomever I choose—carefully—to skewer or commend that evening, dealer's choice. The show's been quite successful, further increasing the station's ratings. That's why Raymond Cook decided I should report directly to him. It was an actual promotion and came with more money—lots more money. Unfortunately, it also came with a closer working relationship between Raymond and me.

I'm not that happy about that part.

I hate his guts, and I'm sure he envies my popularity, although his bottom line loves it. Regardless of how I might feel about it, though, he's still the boss. He gets to call the shots. All of them. And never lets me forget it.

But that's not the only fly in my bourbon.

My former co-anchor, Carly Crown, is seated at my right. She's stunningly elegant in a sapphire blue dress with a plunging neckline that draws the immediate attention of every male in the room. Some females, too. Her blond hair is styled in loose waves and, tonight, looks disturbingly like my wife's. Perhaps she didn't intend it to, but I wouldn't put it past her. Every now and then, her knee rubs against my thigh.

I usually like the seemingly casual interactions, the not-so-accidental touching, the innuendo coloring our conversations at work. But not tonight. Not with a pissed off Amanda seated at my left. I don't want trouble on the home front.

Pulling away, I shoot Carly a warning glance. She veers her eyes toward the empty stage, but there's a certain tension in her lips that tells me I'm going to hear about my distance real soon. And I'm not going to like it. Carly is a death hazard dressed in Pierre Cardin.

The woman across the table stops speaking mid-phrase as the lights in the atrium grow brighter. Raymond climbs onto the stage and grabs the microphone. The light music in the background fades. He clears his voice and coughs into his fist—thankfully, before the mic goes live.

"Thank you all for being here with us tonight in beautiful Malibu. What a fantastic setting for such a noble cause! I hope you enjoyed the delicious meal as much as I did—though I must admit, the dessert might've been a bit too good. If I don't fit into my tux tomorrow, I'll know who to blame!"

The room regales him with a roar of laughter. I can tell the open bar made a difference this year.

"But before the evening comes to an end, there's the moment you've all been waiting for." He pauses for a moment, and the audience stills.

About fucking time.

We've been doing this for four years, and this is the first time he's letting me speak. I straighten my tie knot once more, but refrain from smoothing my hair with my hands. I'm ready.

No, I'm not. I take another sip of bourbon. *Now, I am.*

"She saves lives for a living," Raymond says, gesturing at and looking in Amanda's direction. The limelight follows his lead and finds us. My wife smiles shyly and bows her head. "As a critical care nurse working the endless battlefields of impaired driving, she's the first one to see the carnage. She will tell you that not everyone makes it, even if Sunset Valley Medical Center's Trauma Unit is one of the best in the nation. She has witnessed, time and again, the heartbreak a split-second bad decision can bring upon families."

He pauses for a moment, then shifts his focus to me. "He is a trusted voice in our community, bringing us the news with integrity and dedication. You know him well; you welcome him into your homes at dinnertime. And before you turn on the news to hear of yet another tragedy that has bloodied the streets of Los Angeles, he hears of it first. He investigates, uncovers the truth, and delivers it to you with all of the shocking details." It's my turn to smile and nod in acknowledgement. "Together, they are a beautiful couple, partnering to play a pivotal role in our organization's success and drive critical change in legislation, with your help. Please welcome Amanda and Paul Davis, ladies and gentlemen!"

My wife and I stand as the audience starts applauding. Beaming, Carly chooses that moment to step up into our limelight and hug me, as if we're at the Oscars or something. She lingers in the hug, filling my nostrils with her scent, grinding her hip against me. I pull away discreetly, knowing all cameras are trained on us. Then, I offer Amanda an arm that she quickly takes as we walk toward the makeshift stage.

She stands by my side at the lectern when I take the mic. The crowd quiets down looking at me, and I love it. "Thank you all for being here tonight. Before we get into the serious stuff, I wanted to share a little joke I heard recently: Why did the reporter sit on the teleprompter?" A pause for effect. "Because they wanted to stay on top of the news!"

The audience laughs heartily, and I bask in it. Then, as the response subsides, I continue. "Alright, now that we've had a laugh, let me tell you a story." I look at my wife, and she nods almost imperceptibly. "About how we started *Citizens Against Impaired Driving*, and, most of all, why. It was when we both realized that our jobs had too much death in them. For Amanda, it was the lives that the amazing team at Sunset Valley couldn't save. Senseless deaths that could've been avoided. For me, it was the litany of incidents I had to bring to you via the news I delivered, every single night. Not a day of respite in our lives and yours; not a day of not having to talk about yet another horrifying 'accident' happening here in LA." I allow a beat of silence to pass so my message can sink in. "It just has to stop. And you can make it happen. *We* can make it happen. Together."

As I say those words, the last of them being drowned by enthusiastic applause, my throat scorches for a drink. At a table close to the podium, the beauty in the backless red dress smiles at me.

I make eye contact and hold it for a moment. Her smile blooms, her head tilting slightly as she throws me a loaded look.

For a moment, I forget about Amanda.

Who knows what the evening might still bring? It's looking good for now.

Like *A Beautiful Couple?*

LESLIE WOLFE

Her husband killed someone.

She's the only witness.

A BEAUTIFUL COUPLE

Buy it now!

ABOUT THE AUTHOR

Meet Leslie Wolfe, bestselling author and mastermind behind gripping thrillers that have won the hearts of over three million readers worldwide. She brings a fresh and invigorating touch to the thriller genre, crafting compelling narratives around unforgettable, powerhouse women.

You might know her from the Detective Kay Sharp series or have been hooked by Tess Winnett's relentless pursuit of justice. Maybe you've followed the dynamic duo Baxter & Holt through the gritty streets of Las Vegas or plunged into political intrigue with Alex Hoffmann.

Recently, Leslie published *The Girl You Killed*, a psychological thriller that's pure, unputdownable suspense. This standalone novel will have fans of *The Undoing*, *The Silent Patient*, and *Little Fires Everywhere* on the edge of their seats.

Whether you're into the mind games of *Criminal Minds*, love crime thrillers like James Patterson's, or enjoy the heart-pounding tension in Kendra Elliot and Robert Dugoni's mysteries, Leslie's got a thriller series for you. Fans of action-packed writers like Tom Clancy or Lee Child will find plenty to love in her Alex Hoffmann series.

Wolfe's latest psychological thriller, *A Beautiful Couple*, will have you racing through the pages gasping for breath until the final jaw-dropping twist, delighting fans of *Gone Girl* and *The Girl on the Train*.

Discover all of Leslie's works on Amazon.com/LeslieWolfe. Want a sneak peek at what's next? Become an insider for early access to previews of her new novels, each a thrilling ride you won't want to miss.

BOOKS BY LESLIE WOLFE

STANDALONE TITLES

A Beautiful Couple
The Surgeon
The Girl You Killed
The Hospital
If I Go Missing
Stories Untold
Love, Lies and Murder

TESS WINNETT SERIES

Dawn Girl
The Watson Girl
Glimpse of Death
Taker of Lives
Not Really Dead
Girl With A Rose
Mile High Death
The Girl They Took
The Girl Hunter

DETECTIVE KAY SHARP SERIES

The Girl From Silent Lake
Beneath Blackwater River
The Angel Creek Girls
The Girl on Wildfire Ridge
Missing Girl at Frozen Falls

BAXTER & HOLT SERIES

Las Vegas Girl
Casino Girl
Las Vegas Crime

ALEX HOFFMANN SERIES

Executive
Devil's Move
The Backup Asset
The Ghost Pattern
Operation Sunset

For the complete list of books in all available formats, visit:
Amazon.com/LeslieWolfe